MW00935060

Huntress Born

Wolf Legacy, Volume 1

Aimee Easterling

Published by Wetknee Books, 2017.

HUNTRESS BORN

First edition. September 17, 2017.

Copyright © 2017 Aimee Easterling.

ISBN: 1976173566

Written by Aimee Easterling.

Chapter 1

I stepped off the bus into a darkened city full of human muggers, territorial werewolves, and countless other scoundrels. But I was prepared. I'd brought cupcakes.

Unfortunately, it wasn't yet time to *eat* those cupcakes. Instead, I keyed an Uber request into my phone with one hand while dragging my rolling suitcase clear of the massive wheels with the other. Then I froze as my inner animal abruptly straightened onto full alert.

Wolf. The hint of fur, musk, and testosterone warred for pride of place with urban odors, and I found myself turning in a tight circle in search of the source of the barely present aroma. If my inner beast wasn't mistaken—and she rarely was—then this wasn't merely a shifter in human form sliding seamlessly through the city streets the way I hoped to do. No, a fur-form werewolf was nearby, running four-legged in a space where only two-leggers belonged.

Hairs lengthened on the backs of my arms as my inner beast responded to danger by requesting ownership of our shared body. We were female, far from our pack, and boasted no recourse save our own lupine fangs. It was time to pull out those ivory weapons and show this stranger how capable we were of fighting back.

But instead of obliging my animal's request, I merely stalked to the edge of the lighted circle that marked the bus drop-off zone. Then, drawing extra sensory assistance from my inner wolf, we peered together into the asphalt shadows.

Drip. Drip. Drip. Even in human form, it was easy to pick out the staccato beat of a leaky faucet inside the closed Greyhound station behind our back. Grumbling cars rolled past one block over while human laughter emanated from what smelled like a bar further down the street. But nothing pointed to danger more severe than tired businessmen enjoying a night out on the town. Nothing suggested that my initial impulse—the urge to track down a wolf who possessed the scent signature of a stalker—was anything more than inexperienced-traveler jitters.

This is unknown territory, I reminded myself. *Maybe smelling a wolf here is no big deal.*

After all, there were several hundred times as many people per square mile in this city compared to the rural enclave where I'd grown up. Presumably, there were several hundred times as many werewolves too.

Still, given the legal imperative against displaying our animal skins to the one-body world, surely it made no sense for a werewolf to be wandering these city streets on four furry feet. No sense...unless the shifter in question was hunting a very specific sort of prey.

Prey like me.

Back home, I would have responded to imminent danger by shifting and running for higher ground. In the process, I'd tug at the pack bond that sat invisible yet ever-present at my fingertips then would laugh with exhilaration as dozens of uncles and aunts and cousins came sprinting up to join me. Together, we'd been known to roust troublesome werewolves away from our borders in less time than it took to whip up a batch of buttercream frosting.

Here though, I was deep in the heart of Greenbriar territory, an invader rather than a defender...from a legal standpoint at least. I had no permission to be present. No permission to walk these streets in search of the brother I'd never before met and who I only hoped was still alive. As such, the smart response would have been to keep my head down and to stay out of trouble. I couldn't go haring off after a total stranger based on nothing more than a whim combined with a trick of the light.

Chase him. Find him, my inner beast countered. She urged me to blow off human worries and slip into the skin of our wolf. To follow our instincts and run. *Now*, she added impatiently.

But before we could duke out our disagreement, the distinctive odor of wolf began receding into the distance. Within seconds, the hint of fur had faded to nothing, hidden beneath the overwhelming aromas of rotting garbage and over-applied perfume.

Perhaps the danger had never been present in the first place other than in my own over-tired brain.

And as the scent trail dissipated, I was once again left alone in a strange city with only a few possessions at my disposal. A suitcase, four cupcakes, and a phone that promised connection to my beloved pack mates. The combination would have to be enough.

THE UBER APP REPORTED that my ride was still several miles out and my stomach ached with the enforced distance from pack. So I sank down onto the curb and succumbed to that most lupine of yearnings—the necessity of calling home.

"Ember." The voice of my father—who wasn't biologically related but who *was* very much my alpha—crept over me like the scent of a newly mown meadow. Shoulders that had hunched up around my ears for the last eighteen hours drifted gradually downward and I eyed the cupcake bin strapped to the top of my suitcase with renewed longing.

Not yet, I chided myself. Hearing Wolfie say my name might have made me feel at home, but I hadn't actually reached a safe harbor. Which meant it wasn't time for my much-anticipated treat. Not quite yet.

"Dad," I answered instead, trying to sound like a capable twenty-five-year-old woman rather than like a scared little girl. Despite my fanged alter-ego, this was the first time I'd left Haven under my own volition. No wonder I felt as jumpy as a newborn colt.

And my father must have sensed the worry imbuing that lone word. Because he dove right into the heart of the issue with all the single-mindedness of a born wolf. "Trouble?" he asked.

"Nothing I can't handle." My tone was firm but I knew Wolfie heard the lie in my voice as easily as I'd picked out the pride and affection in his. So I strove to make the next sentence true by recalling the way the scent of fur had faded almost as soon as it entered my nostrils. "I'm fine," I added, focusing on the fact that the trouble really was gone. I *had* handled the potential problem. So my initial words weren't really a falsehood after all.

And the evasion seemed to work. Unfortunately, my father moved on to a question that was much harder to sidestep. "Are you eating your cupcake yet?" Wolfie asked next, his deep rumble the lupine equivalent of a relaxing purr.

This time I hesitated, unwilling to fudge a question so tightly tied to a beloved childhood ritual. Because Dad had been baking gift cupcakes ever since I'd reached my teens, using the unique pastries to celebrate hurdles overcome and milestones achieved. In today's case, the pastry Wolfie had concocted with his own two hands—unlike the more numerous ones I'd made myself—was tucked away deep within my suitcase, a single-serving bin hiding what was bound to be a work of art.

I hadn't even seen my present yet. Was saving that particular boost for the moment when I was finally able to let down my guard and relax into my bed tonight. I wanted to eat the gift with care while feeling the pack bond encircle me just like my father's arms had done so many times before. I wanted to use Dad's cupcake to remember I was loved.

So, in the end, I didn't even attempt a lie as I answered my father's second question of the evening. "Not yet," I admitted. Then, remembering my supposed independence and the very real distance separating me from my home pack, I added: "But you can go to sleep anyway. I have this covered."

Wolfie hummed acknowledgement of my honesty, but that didn't mean he was willing to let me off the hook just yet. "If you're not eating, then I'm not sleeping," my father murmured, his words warming my belly far more than a mere morsel of chocolate might have done.

But then the silence between us turned brittle, and I sighed, knowing which often-repeated conversation was coming next. "You don't have to say it," I interjected, cutting my father off at the pass. "This might be a wild-goose chase and Derek might not want to be found. If my brother really intended to get to know me, he would have come to visit in person rather than sending cryptic messages that resulted in me crossing territory lines. That all makes just as much sense as it did the first time you said it...but I'm willing to take the chance. I can't leave my brother dangling if he's really in trouble."

"I know," Dad rumbled, his voice just as warm now as it had been a moment earlier. He didn't correct my semantics, either. Didn't mention that Derek was only a half-brother or that our shared mom had chosen to abandon me at birth. Instead, Dad's next words proved that my adopted father, at least, would always be on my side even if he disapproved of my current actions. "That wasn't what I was going to say at all."

The phone went silent as my father paused, and I closed my eyes to better sense his presence. Despite the hundreds of miles that separated us, merely breathing in tandem revitalized exhausted muscles and soothed traveling jitters. I would have gladly sat there all night, soaking up Wolfie's strength and reveling in the connection of pack.

But I had places to go. Brothers to meet. Alphas to charm. So, at last, I prodded my father back onto track. "Dad?"

Immediately, Wolfie's deep rumble filled my ears once again. "No matter what happens, Buttercup, I'll be here to back you up. You can always come home."

A human twenty-something would have responded with an agitated eye roll. There were even some shifters who might have felt stifled by an adopted parent's clear obsession with their continued well-being.

But I wasn't one of the latter. For me, family was everything. As such, I had every intention of finding the half-brother I'd never before met, making sure he wasn't in trouble, then high-tailing it back the way I'd come as quickly and carefully as possible.

Unfortunately, now wasn't the time to bask in familial reassurances. Because the scent of fur had returned, filling the air more strongly than ever. And this time, it was all I could do to swallow down a lupine growl.

"I've gotta go," I said instead, disconnecting the call without waiting for a reply and slipping my phone into a pants pocket for safekeeping. Then clambering to my feet, I stared out into the darkness in search of a wolf.

Chapter 2

When the stranger emerged from the shadows at last, an inexperienced human would have found him inconsequential. His lupine belly nearly scraped the pavement and each step was placed more cautiously than the last, producing the impression of an abused and tentative stray dog.

But, to a shifter, the threat was obvious. This wolf wasn't skittishly searching for a handout. He was exercising the careful moderation of a practiced hunter. And, as the only living being within eye shot, I was definitely the one who'd been earmarked as prey.

Opening my mouth, I rolled a great gulp of air across my taste buds in an effort to analyze the stranger's threat level. He wasn't particularly dominant—I could smell that much from a distance. But despite his lack of alpha oomph, the male was crouched in readiness to spring while his teeth were plenty long enough to take down an average human.

Luckily, I was neither average nor human.

"I'm Ember Wilder-Young," I said loudly, taking one long step forward as the stranger paused at the edge of the slim circle of illumination provided by the streetlight above my head. A werewolf shouldn't have needed excessive volume to pick out words across the distance that separated us. But I opted to raise my voice anyway, mimicking the firm yet gentle dominance my father had embodied for my entire life. "I've got a ride coming and your alpha's expecting me. So there's no need to wait around. I'm good."

I seemed to be telling everyone that I was good today...and no one was willing to take my assertion at face value either. Like Wolfie, this shifter snorted out a huff of air that called my sanity into question. But then he lifted his muzzle and inhaled deeply through his moist, black nose.

I could see the moment the stranger caught my scent. The breeze, such as it was, had been blowing in the opposite direction from the beginning or this wolf would have gathered all salient details before even stepping out of the shadows. Now he froze, head cocked to one side as he tried to figure out how a woman like me came to be in a place like this.

"You smell like rich, irresistible chocolate to any red-blooded shifter male," one of my cousins had told me the day before. *"You're nuts to leave pack lands unprotected."*

Other family members had chimed in with similar admonitions, trying to keep me at home where I was safe. But I had reasons to be here and I definitely wasn't going to let the first starry-eyed shifter with more libido than sense send me scurrying back to Haven with my tail between my legs.

So I stood my ground as the wolf drifted closer, his eyes gleaming and the first hint of slobber trailing across pink gums. *Yuck.* Apparently even the mention of an absent alpha wasn't enough to get me off the hook this time around. Time to come up with a plan B.

Let me, my wolf murmured underneath my skin. She wanted to speak with my tongue, to order the less dominant wolf to stand down. The compulsion would have worked, too...and yet I hesitated, shifting nervously from foot to foot rather than reaching for our most obvious line of defense.

Because I'd learned the hard way that bending a weaker wolf around my little finger with a simple verbal command wasn't as painless as it appeared from the dominant side. Instead, being controlled by a stronger shifter was akin to listening to nails scrape across a blackboard while watching someone vomit out great big gobs of stinky stomach contents...all while dangling upside down over a deep abyss that ended in a trough of voracious alligators. There was no long-term damage associated with the compulsion, but the ordeal itself was certainly unpleasant in the moment.

So, yes, I could bark this growling shifter into line...but should I? What if my initial impression had been wrong and the male wasn't busy stalking women who'd made the unfortunate mistake of walking alone at night? What if I was merely on edge from my recent trip and this male intended to remind me not to traipse through someone else's territory without permission?

When in doubt, don't, I decided, opting against forcing my opponent to back down the easy way. Instead, I stood a little taller and gazed directly into the wolf's greenish eyes. "You really don't want to mess with me," I promised too quietly for a human to hear.

Then, relaxing my hold over my own inner beast, I allowed the stranger to see a hint of the animal hidden beneath my human skin.

She might have been smaller than my opponent's animal, but my wolf was no lightweight. Instead, she was twice as dominant as our aggressor, twice as able to stand up for herself in either a physical or verbal battle. As intimidation tactics went, showing a glimpse of her behind my eyes was akin to a war-like nation threatening to drop an atomic bomb.

And, sure enough, plan C worked like a charm. Drool dried up in an instant as the shifter swiveled without a sound. Then he was heading back into the shadows from which he'd come, not a single yip of protest reaching my ears.

There was nothing like a stronger force to make a budding bully back down.

"And my Uber's almost here too," I noted, glancing down at my phone. I'll admit my voice was a little smug as I watched headlights flicker across the wall behind me. Already, I was thinking three steps in advance, counting my remaining cupcakes as I imagined doling them out to each person I'd need to charm before I could lay my head on a pillow and drift into rejuvenating sleep.

One for the Uber driver, one for the Greenbriar pack leader, one for my eventual host. Luckily, I had precisely three cupcakes left...not counting my own treat smashed between clean undies and a work blouse, that is. *Perfect.*

Which is when I picked up a sound from the direction in which the wolf had fled. A wolf's growl. A woman's gasp.

Meanwhile, the air around me filled with the sharp scent of overwhelming fear. Perhaps I shouldn't have given that wolf so much benefit of the doubt after all....

MY INITIAL IMPULSE was to take off in search of my erstwhile companion, but the oncoming vehicle had already purred to a halt before I could make my move. And as I stood eying the expanse of sleek, shiny metal, a tinted window rolled down to reveal a man twice as beautiful as the hunk of steel that surrounded him.

"You called an Uber?" the driver asked, sable hair floating down to partially obscure equally dark and mysterious eyes. Despite myself, I leaned in closer to harvest a sniff. Soap, smarts, confidence. The scent was intoxicating.

The driver was human, though, which in this era of extreme shifter secrecy meant he was also entirely off limits. Forcing my head away from the open window, I bit my lip and squashed the hum of lupine interest threatening to rise up through my human throat. Never mind the rules—there was no point in considering a relationship with a one-body when I had no intention of mating outside my pack.

My wolf whimpered within my stomach, chastened by the reminder. But it was the muffled shriek—just distant enough to be indiscernible to a normal human—that pulled me back to the present with a jolt. "I forgot something down there," I said hurriedly before twisting my arm to gesture awkwardly at the suitcase by my feet. "Help yourself to a cupcake," I added, "and I'll be right back."

Hoping the treat would keep my driver occupied while he waited, I took off at a run just barely slow enough to appear human. Then even that pretense fell away as shadows settled around my furless skin and shielded me from view. I'd made one mistake already in letting the stranger off scot-free. I had no intention of allowing him to harm a human on my watch.

Still, even as I raced down the dark alley intent upon rescue, my mind was attempting to assemble a puzzle whose pieces didn't quite add up. I was new to this city and unfamiliar with local customs, but it made no sense for a shifter to be attacking females willy-nilly. After all, the Greenbriar alpha would be acting under the same mandate that guided Dad's governance—the imperative to keep the peace within his pack while also ensuring werewolves remained hidden from prying human eyes. Moral implications aside, Chief Greenbriar would have to be an idiot to allow underlings to draw attention to themselves by breaking one-body laws.

Shivering despite the warmth of the night, I allowed my wolf to rise up and join me within our human skin at last. *She* wasn't concerned about the inconsistencies presented by this city's rotten underbelly. Instead, her attention latched onto the renegade werewolf who'd cornered a human woman in the shadowy enclave between a metal dumpster and an unyielding brick wall.

Despite the darkness, my shifter senses made the scene all too clear. And I winced as I realized the attacker had taken yet another step into the unthinkable during the moments he'd spent alone. Because he wasn't a wolf now. Instead, the male was two-legged and naked, presumably having transformed right in front of the young woman he was currently attempting to maul.

Unsavory repercussions flew in front of my mind's eye in one jumbled heap. There was no wiggle room in this particular law. No way to save a human who had been privy to a shifter's transition from wolf to man. Instead, if this woman had been able to discern her attacker's shift despite the darkness...well then, she'd have to be killed for the sake of werewolves everywhere.

I'd just have to hope the woman's eyesight wasn't up to the task.

The victim didn't need night vision, though, to be terrified. Not when her attacker had ripped open the front of her blouse, his other hand fumbling with the buttons of her jeans. "You're fertile," the male murmured, his words more wolf than human. "Ripe, round, ready."

And despite my former intentions not to make waves, I abruptly saw red. This wasn't the way werewolves acted. Forget the mandate not to show ourselves in public, this was *uncivilized*.

Uncle Hunter would have punched out the attacker's lights. Dad would have shifted into lupine form and torn into this stranger with tooth and claw. Right now, either option seemed like a good one to me.

But stumbling footsteps in the alley behind my back marked the approach of my Uber driver, his advance slow but steady. Darn his cute face, the guy was too chivalrous to allow me to be assaulted in a dark alley on his watch.

Which meant, unfortunately, I didn't have the wiggle room to assault anyone in a dark alley either.

So, instead, I readied the talent I'd rejected earlier as akin to killing a mosquito with a sledgehammer. This time around, I figured the bug in question deserved to be squished. *"Go home,"* I ordered, my voice too quiet for either human to hear.

The stranger, though, not only heard but *felt*. Predictably, he jerked like a puppet whose stage manager had pulled the strings and bade him to dance. But the shifter didn't flee immediately. Instead, the bastard tried to fight against my overt command, swiveling around to glare at me over one naked shoulder as he fought against the compulsion to obey.

Then the Uber driver was in the alley behind us. His flashlight shone across the wall and dumpster before glinting against the woman's eyes...and that was all the illumination the latter needed to raise the canister of Mace she'd been clutching in one white-knuckled grip and spray it directly into her attacker's face.

My shifter dominance would have done the trick eventually...but I have to admit the effects of pepper spray were far more satisfying. Because the attempted rapist yowled as if his victim had stuck a knife through his groin. Then he was running down the alley in the opposite direction, air humming with electricity as he shifted into lupine form just out of sight.

Breathing a sigh of relief, I crossed my fingers and hoped the two humans didn't realize they'd just sighted the impossible—a person able to transform into the body of a wolf at will. Because if they put two and two together, the law said I had to put them down.

I definitely didn't have enough cupcakes on hand to deal with that sort of catastrophe.

Chapter 3

To my relief, neither human appeared to notice anything beyond the obvious—that a terrified woman had finally found safety once her attacker was chased away. My luck continued to hold, too, when the victim made it all the way to the sleek sports car before collapsing into a tearful heap in the leather-lined safety of the small back seat.

The female didn't respond to any of my condolences, though, suggesting that she needed a little time to collect herself. So, after offering yet another unnoticed pat on the back, I glanced up and caught the Uber driver's gaze in the side mirror instead.

In stark contrast to my own suitcase-top perch outside the car's open door, the driver was visibly distancing himself from the feminine gaggle behind his back. Not that I blamed him—he probably needed to get back to making a living. Figuring it was only fair to let him off the hook, I smiled grimly and offered the driver an easy way out.

"I'm sorry," I began. "I think this is gonna take a while. It won't hurt my feelings at all if you need to go find another fare...."

And in response, a wave of emotion so intense I could smell it from outside the car flickered across the driver's chiseled face. "Are you serious? You think I'm going to leave you two here alone in the middle of the night when there's a potential rapist on the loose?"

The male's tone was as curt as any alpha werewolf who thought his pack mates were in danger. And despite the driver's complete inability to change forms, testosterone sizzled through the air while barely banked rage attempted to break through his cool facade.

Huh, guess I had him pegged all wrong. Here I'd thought my driver was irritated and uncomfortable with the crying woman parked in his back seat. Instead, the human was furious about the events that had come before. In fact, I got the distinct impression he wanted nothing more than a chance to pound that potential rapist into the pavement.

Well, that makes two of us.

As quickly as the rage appeared, though, the man's face smoothed and I was left wondering if I'd merely imagined the strength of his former reaction. "I'm here for the duration," the driver continued, twisting his body sideways and reaching into the space between the seat and door so he could shake my hand. "So I guess I might as well introduce myself. I'm Sebastien Carter...and you're Ember Wilder-Young."

"How...?" I asked, the human's firm grip short-circuiting my already weary brain. Close up, Sebastien's odor enveloped me like a warm hug, the faint addition of sandalwood-scented sweat lingering beneath his more signature aromas. My companion smelled like adventure and danger and hidden potential...and I wanted to transform into a wolf so I could jump into his lap and lick his square-jawed face.

Releasing the large hand a tad too quickly for the sake of politeness, awareness fled in an instant as my usual perspicuity returned. Of course my name would have been listed on the user profile when I requested a ride. There was nothing magical about an Uber driver knowing who I was.

"And I'm Harmony Garcia," the woman beside me interjected, straightening at long last in response to our more-intimate-than-intended exchange. As I finally got a good look at her, I realized that she must have been on her way home from work despite the late hour. Because a black pant suit hugged her trim curves while carefully applied mascara remained pristine despite her recent sob-fest.

Impressive on both counts. Perhaps I'd underestimated the average human woman's inherent spine.

Still, even with the steely inner strength Harmony displayed, recent shock pinched the corners of her lips and grayed her skin. She needed a little boost to fully brush off the close call with a werewolf. Good thing I had just the ticket right here on top of my suitcase....

The woman's lips curled upward into a hint of a smile as I silently offered the cupcake carton in one outstretched hand. And after perusing the selection with all the intensity of a stock analyst choosing where to invest her retirement income, Harmony plucked out the strawberry-flavored confection I'd made with someone very much like her in mind.

Now it was my turn to grin as Harmony inhaled half the pastry in one great gulp before leaning back against the seat with a sigh of relief. *Success.* My greatest weapon—the mighty cupcake—had come through at last.

FIGURING HARMONY WOULD fare even better if not forced to eat alone, I held out the nearly empty carton to Sebastien next. And to my surprise, the Uber driver plucked the triple-chocolate overload rather than the raspberry-crumble I'd figured would be in his wheelhouse.

Huh. We both have the same favorite flavor? What are the chances of that?

But before I could verbalize my surprise, the chime of my phone reminded me that I had far more important matters on my agenda than psychoanalyzing humans based on their cupcake selections. Because even though the name on the screen—"Top Dog"—wasn't one I recognized, the associated text message sent a shiver running down my spine.

No greeting, no small talk. Just a street address and a deadline. *Midnight*, the final word read, curtness evident in the truncated command.

Reading between the lines, I could only assume that my hosts had noticed my uninvited presence in Greenbriar territory far sooner than I'd anticipated. I'd considered calling ahead and using diplomacy to find a legal way into this city, but in the end had decided it was better to ask forgiveness rather than permission.

Actually, I'd kinda hoped I could find my brother and hop back onto the bus before anyone was the wiser. No harm, no foul. Perhaps I'd send Chief Greenbriar a fruit basket once I was safely back in Haven.

Only that wishful-thinking bubble now burst like a Yorkshire pudding falling flat as soon as the pan left the oven. Chief Greenbriar had discovered my intrusion far faster than I'd estimated. And now I possessed twenty short minutes to achieve the lair of this region's alpha before my neck would be on the chopping block...perhaps quite literally.

Despite the need for speed, I felt a strange aversion to the idea of running off and leaving these humans behind. Instead, I watched wistfully as the color returned to Harmony's cheeks while the male in the driver's seat leaned inward to shield her body from imagined danger. *Strawberry and chocolate go well together*, I reminded myself, ignoring the flutter of disappointment that rose in my chest at the very thought of leaving my Uber driver to take the other female home.

Still, I did what had to be done. Snapping the nearly empty cupcake container back into place, I yanked up on the handle of my suitcase in preparation for making tracks.

But I wasn't quite quick enough. Sebastien's door opened and his large hand clamped down around my luggage-handling wrist before I even saw him coming. The guy was nearly werewolf fast.

"Where do you think you're going?" the male demanded.

"Sorry about the fare, but I just realized I'm running late," I answered, words tumbling all over themselves in their rush to exit my mouth. "If you don't mind, can you take Harmony home and charge the trip to the credit card I have on file?" Then, glancing backwards at the aforementioned female, I added, "It was a pleasure to meet you! Have a good night."

Finally, I pulled away, thoroughly expecting Sebastien's hand to fall free as I exerted myself. But instead, I found myself swinging back around to face the human, his iron grip refusing to budge. "No," he said simply.

My brows drew together. Really? Dude thought he could keep me from going where I wanted to go?

And even though I was predisposed to like anyone who opted for a chocolate cupcake, muscle memory took over as soon as I found myself restrained. Dropping my weight into a semi-squat, I bent my elbow and pushed forward with all of my might.

Sure enough, Sebastien grunted and let go. In a contest between muscles and skillful use of physics, physics won out every time.

Thank you, Uncle Hunter, I thought silently, ignoring the grumbling of my wolf at the less-than-savory parting.

But I had no time to apologize, no time to make nice with the humans. Instead, turning on my heel, I ran down the sidewalk into the night.

Chapter 4

Despite my haste, I paused just out of sight and listened until the murmur of voices ceased and two car doors slammed shut. Sure enough, Harmony had accepted Sebastien's offer of assistance, her throaty voice reciting a street address that I quickly keyed into my own phone...just in case.

Then my human companions were gone and I was left to chart a course through the unfamiliar neighborhood by myself. And even though the mapping software on my phone would have come in handy to ensure I made no wrong turns on the way to my intended destination, my gut told me I'd be better off taking this trek unencumbered. So I made a short pit stop first.

Heaving my suitcase into a storage locker in the antechamber of the bus station, I then emptied my pockets until all I had on me was a t-shirt and jeans. Even my phone went into the keypad-locked metal box, the gesture essential if I didn't want to be tracked by a shifter who had already found a way to hack into my supposedly untappable phone.

The mystery of that cleverness would have to wait, though. Instead, I slithered up a tree, scampered across a balcony, then chinning my way onto a low rooftop that would serve as a stepping stone to those levels higher up. This part of the city was so densely packed that it was feasible to turn buildings themselves into an aerial pathway...as long as I didn't mind making running leaps over alleys from time to time, that was.

My wolf definitely wasn't fazed by the necessary loss of contact with the earth. In fact, I barely managed to squash her howl as we embraced freedom together, sprinting across the wide open spaces and stretching legs that had been pent-up within the squashed confines of that dratted bus for far too long. The ability to run unfettered was pure bliss.

After a few seconds, though, we got back down to business. Beneath our feet, humans clomped by entirely unaware that a predator could drop down upon them at any moment, and I had high hopes that any nearby shifters were equally oblivious to my current MO. Still, I wasted a few precious minutes looping the loop until I was certain no one trailed my current movements or accidentally stumbled across my path.

Only then did I dig into my memory of the city's map and begin making my way toward the location Top Dog had ordered me to attend. My destination was relatively close by....but I still began second-guessing my own navigational abilities as I neared Top Dog's designated intersection.

Because this wasn't the wealthy and polished neighborhood I'd expect to find housing an alpha werewolf. There were no park-like expanses of trees, no fenced mansions to keep prying eyes at bay. Instead, human hookers posed on street corners while boys far too young to be out and about so late at night sold small baggies of illicit substances to an endless stream of easy marks.

As I passed unnoticed above all of their heads, a clock tower tolled proof that my evasive maneuvers had already put me behind the designated hour. I'd need to apologize for my tardiness now as well as my cheekiness in arriving unannounced...but who was supposed to grant me amnesty when I hadn't smelled a single shifter since leaving the bus station behind?

Then I saw them. Three wolves lounging beneath a basketball hoop where the streetlights just happened not to shine. Gray fur blended easily into the silver moonlight, explaining why they felt safe walking four-legged while one-bodies worked nearby. Their camouflage was good. Still, I suspected Dad wouldn't have allowed this level of overt wolfishness to fly.

But threats to shifter secrecy weren't the largest issue currently on the table. I'd hoped to keep roof-running as a backup plan in case the upcoming meeting went south, but the wind was out to get me. Even as I began planning a circuitous descent, a gust of summer trickery carried my scent down toward the pavement. And as one the trio tilted their heads to peer upwards into the dark.

I'd been sighted. Now, there was no going back.

I HESITATED, CONSIDERING flight for one short second. But my brother was still out there, somewhere, waiting for me to answer his digital plea. And I had other aces up my sleeve even if the roof was no longer my personal playground.

So, using an awning to slow my descent, I landed gracefully on two human feet even as strange wolves came padding up to greet me.

Okay, so perhaps "greet" wasn't the right verb. Instead, as soon as I hit the ground, the pack was chivying me deeper into the shadows and further away from human eyes. The largest male led the way while others nipped at my heels, brushing against my legs hard enough to make me stumble.

"You don't have to be so pushy," I grumbled under my breath, nonetheless picking up my heels as we all padded away from the more trafficked street corner at a ground-eating trot.

The only response to my complaint was another bite, and this time the wolf in question didn't bother to exercise restraint. Instead, his sharp teeth tore through the fabric of my jeans, making me wince as the metallic tang of blood rose to permeate the warm evening air.

Just what I needed—to excite these predators further with the scent of flowing blood.

True to form, the lead animal immediately dropped all pretense at stealth, raising his chin to the sky and howling into the night. Luckily, by this point the neighborhood we were traveling through had changed from inner city to well-heeled gentry, which meant the residents were all tucked away snug in their beds. Hopefully no one heard the truncated howl...or the more elongated scuffle as three impatient wolves herded a mostly-willing human down the pavement beside an endless string of night-darkened homes.

Only there weren't only three wolves hemming me in any longer. Two others had slipped out of the bushes while I wasn't looking, after which a pair of youngsters pranced up to join the hunt. So there were eight of us, all-told, when we paused at the edge of a busy, two-lane road.

The pups were what prompted me to make it easy for my escort at last. "I assume you want me to go straight on through," I told the leader, who hadn't once glanced over his shoulder since beginning to lead us all on this entirely unnecessary dance. "How about I cross here and you meet me on the other side?" I continued, speaking to ears that swiveled even though the male's snout remained firmly facing the brightly lit pavement twenty yards ahead.

And I must have struck the right tone at last because the male finally turned to face me head-on. I'd assumed from his high-handedness that our leader was an elder, but a glance at his muzzle now proved that he was actually no more than a year or two older than myself.

More important than his age, though, was his mood. Our current leader was understandably annoyed by my recent tardiness, was pissed at having been asked to herd me along in the first place. And yet...the male was currently in lupine form and tuned into the thoughts of an animal rather than to those of a man. As such, a willing addition to the hunt overrode all petty grievances from the already foggy past.

Soon enough, the leader's eyes widened slightly, a request for me to clarify my recent words. And, willingly, I repeated my offer. "I'm not here to cause trouble. I'll follow wherever you lead."

I'd expected perhaps a nod of acceptance or a snarl of retort. Instead, in a strange burst of inclusiveness, a temporary pack bond settled across my shoulders, attaching me to wolves I barely knew. I could feel not only these shifters waiting impatiently on the street corner, but also members of the pack not currently present who—I now knew—were running toward us along other darkened city streets.

The sensation was scratchy and uncomfortable, blocking me off from more familiar connections to my father and home clan while tying me to strangers I'd never even met. And while

I wouldn't have wanted to keep a Greenbriar mantle in place for very long, its current presence was welcome nonetheless.

Because being tied into the local network meant an end to backbiting and herding. An end to the skepticism that filled the air like the scent of moldy bread. This Greenbriar leader didn't precisely trust me, and I also hadn't tied myself so thoroughly to the other shifters that I couldn't veer away at will. Despite those caveats, we were all in total agreement. For tonight, at least, we'd chosen each other's company for the upcoming run.

Chapter 5

As soon as the decision was made, we were off. Wolf-form shifters slipped away into the shadows, darting down alleys before reappearing atop an unlit bridge that crossed the thoroughfare two blocks away. For my part, human feet carried me more sedately across the closest intersection and I nodded at a policeman before picking up my heels on the opposite side. *Just a human, out for a run*, I told the official with the relaxed set of my shoulders. And, like most one-bodies, the policeman saw what he expected to see.

On the other side of the avenue, even more wolves settled in around me until I was trotting amidst a sea of fur and paws. The road we were following twisted into seclusion here, trees cropping up as we passed through an abandoned industrial district. Then a vast chain-link fence rose before us just where I'd thought a human park would exist based on my perusal of satellite photos during the long bus ride north.

My assumptions had apparently been flawed, though. Because a shifter waited at the gate, suggesting that this area wasn't open to the public...nor was it frequented by the two-legged set. Unlike the other shifters milling around me, this teenager was in human form. But he was also entirely naked save for an incongruously orange pair of flip-flops that slid around his otherwise bare feet with every step.

"Welcome to the Greenbriar pack," the male told me, swinging open the gates then standing back as the flood of wolves streamed through, jostling against each other in their haste to achieve the wooded side.

I stood back to let them pass but didn't attempt to argue with the gate guard about the temporariness of my recently assumed pack mantle. Instead, I slipped fingers over each shoulder then below my waistband, unsnapping special fasteners I'd added to my underwear after learning that my dominant nature made the upcoming party trick feasible.

Then, as the two-legged shifter who'd let us in began a slow and laborious transition into lupine form, I dove forward...and shifted into wolf so quickly that my trousers and shirt, my panties and bra all fell into a crumpled heap beneath my paws.

Finally, four-legged, I followed the other werewolves into the trees.

CHIEF GREENBRIAR MET us at the top of the highest rise, his grizzled muzzle lined with scars from battles long past. Otherwise, though, his markings were reminiscent of those on the shifter who'd played Pied Piper during my recent journey through town. And as I breathed in similar aromas emanating from either side of me, I realized the two males likely also shared common blood.

Father and son, I decided, noting the way all other wolves dropped to their bellies and lowered their eyes at the sight of their waiting leader. In stark contrast, my guide walked right up and sniffed his alpha's nose without obvious sign of deference. So this wasn't the sort of pack were an heir apparent was required to defend his place ad nauseam. A very good sign.

Too bad I didn't have a cupcake on hand to grease the wheels of my own arrival and prompt similar familiarity. Still, I opted to assume Chief Greenbriar would be a raspberry sort of fellow just like the cupcake I'd saved for him—a bit sour and well able to hold his own amid other flavors, but sugary sweet on the inside.

Testing my hypothesis, I pranced up to the alpha just as I would have to my own father. Then, without waiting to gauge his reaction, I granted the older wolf a playful but deferent lick beneath his furry chin.

My breath caught as the older male's ears pinned back for a millisecond, but then his tongue lolled out in a lupine laugh. Accepting my far-from-formal introduction, he took my head between massive jaws and shook me gently from side to side in a formalized rebuke for my tardiness. But at the same time, the scratchy connection that his son had applied eased into silky smoothness across my back as the strongest alpha in the vicinity approved of my temporary inclusion within his clan.

In stark contrast to the loosely applied mantle that had broadcast nothing more than the pack's shared enthusiasm earlier in the evening, individual reactions now rolled toward me in emotional waves. The two youngest werewolves were full of trepidation, unsure whether they'd show themselves to advantage during their first formal hunt. One adult shifter was hungover, while another harbored annoyance at being required to attend an event that cut into previously scheduled plans.

Despite these few dissonant notes though, most of the wolves were raring to go. They were impatient with the hunt's late start, uninterested in my unexpected presence, and thinking of nothing more than running flat out while cool night breezes wafted through stifling fur.

But the alpha didn't give us permission to begin at once. Instead, he tightened the reins and held us all in check for a long moment until we were stamping like race horses impatient to be off. Then he cocked his head...and gazed directly into my waiting eyes.

I tensed, fully aware that an eye lock like this one would have been a stark challenge among alpha males. But I was female and often capable of wiggling out of dominance battles with an appeasing smile...assuming no handy cupcakes were lying around waiting to be doled out, that is.

This time, though, I didn't even need to resort to feminine wiles in order to defuse the tension. Because Chief Greenbriar wasn't confronting me. Rather, he was assessing, measuring, asking if I'd like to be the one to lead the evening's hunt.

The gesture was still a test, of course, albeit a more palatable one than the stare-down he could have chosen. Definitely far better than I'd expected from a pack leader who had no reason to even allow me to walk his streets unhindered, let alone grant me the honored position of leading a full-pack hunt.

Of course if I failed to find prime prey....

Luckily, I was always up for a challenge. Closing my eyes, I raised my nose as if scenting the breeze, and in the process recalled the maps I'd stared at for hours as the pitifully slow bus paused in each small town along its path.

Based on those images, this fenced-in sanctuary was too small to contain anything more tasty than a doe or two. On the other hand, if the pack headed downhill for a few short miles, we'd come upon an arm of national forest that my research suggested had been stocked with elk decades before.

The large ungulates had done so well for themselves during the intervening period that the state's department of game and inland fisheries had instituted an annual hunting season with the goal of preventing overpopulated elk from wandering down city streets in search of flowerbeds to nibble on.

And if humans were allowed to hunt elk...well perhaps werewolves were too.

Chapter 6

No one argued when I took off to the south. Instead, they fell in line behind me as easily as if I were their usual guide rather than an uninvited guest. And before we'd even reached the limits of the pack's fenced sanctuary, the alpha's son was running by my side, his shoulder bumping playfully against my own.

Well that's a change of tune, I thought wryly. Still, I couldn't blame the younger male for dropping his former aloofness as soon as Chief Greenbriar offered explicit approval of my presence. After all, the city's leader was that rarest of alphas—a male like my father whose profound power meant he had no need to threaten or punish in order to make his pack obey.

By his actions, Chief Greenbriar had suggested I was more important to their pack than anyone had initially suspected. So now his son was wooing me far more seriously than was merited by our short acquaintance.

In response, I played along. Well, not too overtly—after all, the younger male's scent of warm granite and damp clay did nothing for my libido and I had absolutely no intention of formalizing the borrowed Greenbriar mantle by mating within their pack. But I didn't push my hunting companion away either. Instead, I matched him nudge for nudge, even allowing the alpha's son to pull ahead and choose the direction of our travel when the path we were running along split in two.

After all, I'd scented elk in both directions. No reason not to let the heir apparent claim the final prize of leading us all to a feast when my own short-term status meant I had no dog—or, rather, elk—in this race.

Instead, I merely relaxed into the heady sensation of running with a pack. The moon was high, the cool air flowing gently over my hot fur. I wasn't home, I wasn't with family, but I *was* happy.

And then, abruptly, a very different sort of scent froze my feet and reminded me that I wasn't just an uninterested bystander acting as an audience to Greenbriar power plays. Slipping out of the stream of wolves, I padded over to sniff at the earth beneath a straight-trunked walnut, trying to determine whether it was my nose or my mind playing tricks.

The answer was—neither. A wolf had definitely peed here not long ago...which wasn't a big surprise since the hole in the fence we'd passed through half an hour earlier suggested this area was often treated as an addendum to the pack's more official hunting grounds. The identity of the scent-marking wolf, though, raised hairs along the entire length of my spine.

Derek. My brother had been present in this very spot no more than a week earlier. And in the way of wolves, he'd imbued not only his identity but also his mood into the chemicals that laced his urine.

The youngster had been scared. Not outright fleeing from a dangerous pursuer, but skulking as lone wolves tend to do around the periphery of an established pack.

Only Derek hadn't been looking for a way in. He'd been looking for a way back *out.*

I lowered my muzzle closer to the earth, doubting the evidence of my own nose. The facts simply didn't add up. Not when Chief Greenbriar and his son had drawn me into their ranks as adroitly as ever my own father had soothed the fears of time-worn loners and given them a place to call home. I'd arrived in the city late and uninvited, expecting to be chased out of town on a rail. And instead, no one in the host clan had so much as hassled me during the recent race through forested glades.

Pawing at the earth, I whined out my confusion. And, to my surprise, the dusty patch yielded up a more tangible prize.

A key on a chain. And nearly hidden beneath the scents of urine and earth, the faintest aroma of moss still adorned the metallic surface. Derek had definitely been the one to tuck away this offering. Perhaps I could use the clue to track my elusive brother down?

Glancing over one shoulder to see if anyone had noted my absence, I slipped my head through the chain and shook myself until the metal settled down invisibly into my thick lupine fur. I didn't know why Derek had come this way several days earlier. Could find no further indication of why he had been frightened or who might have been hounding his trail.

But my missing sibling had left behind a key. I had to assume that meant I was finally on the proper track.

UNFORTUNATELY, THE mystery of Derek's disappearance would have to wait. Because I could feel the alpha's son racing in for the kill via the borrowed Greenbriar mantle. Meanwhile, a change in the connections streaming between me and the other shifters suggested I was about to lose my chance at making a good impression on this borrowed pack.

Sure enough, when I glanced up, Chief Greenbriar's gaze met mine through gaps in the intervening trees. The older male's eyes narrowed in speculation, and I could almost feel his questions streaming toward me down our temporary pack tether...

...only to be cast aside as a glint of reflected moonlight illuminated the younger Greenbriar male's teeth. Fangs latched onto the loose skin beneath the neck of a tremendous elk, and across the scrimmage the alpha howled his immediate approval. Then both alpha and son were lost from view as a surge of wolves darted past the prey animal's feet, snapping at flanks and belly in an effort to take the elk all the way to the ground.

It was time to join in or be left out entirely, I realized. There needed to be blood on my fangs before this night was over if I wanted permission to hunt in this city ever again.

To that end, I pressed forward, thankful that the wolves on the periphery of the battle so readily allowed me to pass. Well, they all stepped aside...save for one skinny beast whose fur stank of fox-musk and dirty socks.

I recognized the rapist more by scent than by sight. Somehow, I'd assumed Harmony's attacker would materialize into a lone wolf like my brother. After all, who but a packless beast would have the temerity to break such a serious law? The male likely made a living out of skulking around the perimeter of claimed territory, succumbing to gaffes that would eventually get him tossed out on his ear...assuming the pack leader was in a good mood at the time and didn't produce a far more final form of punishment for the indiscretion.

But in this case, the foul-scented male was right in the thick of the action. And unlike his fellow pack members, he didn't budge as I approached. Instead, the shifter remained directly in my path, lip curled and teeth bared in a reminder that not every resident of the city was thrilled by my uninvited presence on their home turf.

I was more surprised by the male's ability to rub shoulders with hunt participants than I was scared of his menacing posture, but my vacillation must have resembled fear from a distance. Because before I could make a move to push the troublesome shifter out of my path, Chief Greenbriar barked out a curt command and his son released the elk's neck with alacrity. Then the younger male was leaping between me and perceived danger, fangs bared and lips curled back as he dove in for the kill.

The battle that ensued felt far harsher and stranger than I would have expected. Snarls soon turned to yelps, and a spray of blood forced me backwards even as I shook my head at the severity of the attack.

This isn't how it's done back home, I couldn't help thinking. Dad would never have turned punishment over to an underling then watched what appeared fated to become a battle to the death.

And even as I backpedaled away from the altercation as quickly as possible, the rest of the pack pushed closer, hemming me in while also providing the formerly beleaguered elk with breathing room in which to make its escape. I only realized I'd been pushed to the outer edge of the circle, in fact, when hooves bit into moss inches away from my unprotected tail, nearly startling me out of my skin.

Whirling, I leapt sideways and found myself spinning up against a female who'd been preparing to dive in the opposite direction. My shoulder knocked against her foreleg and she fell...directly into the retreating ungulate's flight path.

Long legs and blunt teeth prove that elk consider themselves prey rather than predators, but even runners eventually fight back. The beast shrieked at what it must have considered renewed aggression, and one hard hoof kicked out sideways to slam into the female's skull with a sickening crack of keratin against bone.

The wolf beside me fell to the earth as soundlessly as death.

Rushing to the female's side, I leaned down to lick away the blood streaming from a cut across her brow. But before I could make contact, closed eyes opened and teeth snapped shut inches away from my muzzle, proving that the other wolf had no interest in being soothed.

Well, if she can bite, she can walk, I decided. Stepping back, I paused and took in the scene that had, seconds ago, hosted two equally vigorous fights to the death.

The clearing was now silent, the elk gone and the shifter-on-shifter scuffle ended. To no one's surprise except perhaps the lupine underdog, the alpha's son had been triumphant in the latter battle. And now the fox-scented male lay on his back with belly exposed to the heir's sharp teeth.

I held my breath, expecting further carnage to ensue. But after the merest hesitation, the loser reached up to lick the winner's chin. And rather than growling further reprimand, the alpha's son released the latter from his grasp. Just as at Haven, once subdued, the loser was set free.

I overreacted, I decided, releasing my pent-up breath in a gust of relieved air. No one had died, no one had even been seriously wounded. Finally, we could return to the hunt.

Only, Chief Greenbriar wasn't content with the current state of affairs. The alpha's displeasure bent down my spine until my tail tucked between my legs and my ears fell back against my skull. There was no explanation and no warning for his change of heart. Instead, our leader merely lashed out with a heaviness that threatened to split my body in half.

And I wasn't the only one affected. All around the clearing, I could hear my fellows similarly wince and whine. We'd failed to please our alpha. We'd failed the pack. Pain was our reward.

Dropping to my belly, I attempted to escape into the earth. This wasn't how I'd intended the hunt to end. For the third time that evening, I wished I could sweeten up my companions with a bin of distant cupcakes.

Chapter 7

Despite the less-than-auspicious middle of the hunt, we *did* manage to track down a deer in the wee hours before dawn. The lone animal didn't possess enough flesh on its bones to turn snack into feast. Still, the carcass provided a bite of rich, red meat for each of us, the sustenance soothing ruffled tempers and cementing my temporary place in the pack. Good enough.

After that, sleep deprivation caught up with me at last and turned pack-wide jubilation distant and hazy. I lay down nose to tail, flanked on either side by similarly exhausted werewolves...and when I woke, dawn was already coloring the distant horizon while the ground beside me had turned cold and bare.

My host pack was gone.

Shivering, I shook a spray of dew out of my fur as I rose onto furry feet. Someone had taken the time to bury the deer's entrails, bones, and hide, so nothing remained of the previous night's carnage save the jolt of warmth that always lingered in my stomach after enjoying meat in lupine form. Unexpected solitude threatened to extinguish that glow...but then curiosity snapped the sensation back into place with a vengeance.

Because an odd, blocky object poked through the fog at the edge of the tree line. And when I padded closer, I recognized the shape at once. *A suitcase.* My *suitcase.*

Cocking my head to one side, I tried to make sense of finding my own luggage—complete with untouched cupcake container—out in the woods when I'd last stuffed all possessions into a locked metal cage back at the bus station for safekeeping. The realization that Chief Greenbriar had ordered a lackey to trail my footsteps back to the bus terminal and retrieve my possessions froze the last hint of warmth out of my belly. The city pack had by-and-large seemed open and inviting last night...so why would they ditch me, stealing away in silence before delivering a clear warning to beat it out of town?

Meanwhile, the buzz of my phone, slipped into an external pocket of the hand-delivered suitcase, drew me out of my brown study. And, immediately, I winced for a different reason entirely.

Oops. How could I have left my father dangling all night long without checking in? I'd probably scared Wolfie so badly when the borrowed Greenbriar mantle settled onto my back and hid our own connection that he'd likely jumped into his car to drive north and rescue me.

I need to fix that, I thought, preparing to tug on Dad's connection and reassure him the easy way. But when I rolled my shoulder blades experimentally, I was surprised to find the Greenbriar mantle still present and accounted for against my skin. Which meant I couldn't set Wolfie's mind at ease nonverbally, not when another pack's network of connection continued to stifle my own.

On the other hand, when I closed my eyes and sought the threads that bound me to other wolves, a tug in my stomach directed my attention west and proved that I wasn't alone after all. *Dad will have to wait*, I thought, swiveling to face the newcomer even as Chief Greenbriar stepped out of the trees in human form.

"Gretchen forgot to drop off your clothes when she brought the suitcase," the alpha greeted me cordially, holding out carefully folded garments in one long-fingered hand. The gesture was strangely subservient for a pack leader. Still, my companion was walking on two legs while I still boasted four, so perhaps I was missing something that would have been obvious to a two-legged being.

Shifting upward in an effort to tune into my more rational human brain, air turned cooler and damper against bare, furless skin in an instant. And it wasn't only the fog that made me shiver as my companion drew closer. It was Chief Greenbriar's eyes, which roved across my exposed body as if I was a horse at market that he was planning to sell...or to buy.

In response, my hand rose to the chain that still dangled around my neck, clasping the key in one fist a moment too late. But that item wasn't what had caught Chief Greenbriar's attention. Instead, despite shifters' usual casual approach to nudity, the alpha's gaze resembled slaps and pinches as it slipped across my bare breasts, around my innie belly button, and down into the V between my legs. For the first time in my life, I was made to feel naked while...well...naked.

"Thanks for bringing my clothes," I said instead of commenting upon the alpha's faux pas. And in response, my companion's scent strengthened, the hard granite that he shared with his son turning rougher and more abrasive. Chief Green-briar took a single step closer...and I bent to snatch up the plastic container I'd found atop my suitcase, using its rectangular bulk to fend off my companion's further approach.

"I saved you a cupcake," I offered, noting the way water had beaded atop raspberry frosting as humid air adhered to the sugary coating. *Remember your sweet core*, I admonished Chief Greenbriar silently, knowing he wouldn't be able to hear my command.

But it was almost as if the alpha had plucked the words straight out of my mind. "I'll trade you," he said, eyes returning to my face as he slipped the tupperware bin out of my hand and replaced it with a stack of folded fabric. Then, less like a wolf and more like a fine-food connoisseur, the older male took a single particle of pastry into his mouth before allowing his eyelids to drift shut in appreciation. "This is delicious," he said at last around a mouthful of frosting and fluff.

Just like that, the strange energy that had infused the air dissipated without a trace. And the male before me was once again a civilized man rather than a randy wolf.

"I'm a wolf of many talents," I answered, donning clothes far more rapidly than I would have done in the company of any other shifter. My stomach remained queasy, but my fears did ease a trifle...

...Only to return in full force as Chief Greenbriar opened his eyes and pinned me with a steely gaze. "I've decided," he told me, "that you will make the perfect match for my son."

BACK HOME, I WOULD have laughed in the alpha's face. Here and now, I instead felt like I was tuning into the grand finale of a TV series I'd never before watched while surrounded by the show's most ardent and devoted fans.

Because there was no way I planned to tie myself permanently to a Greenbriar werewolf when doing so would cut off the most important part of my life—the bond to my home pack. Of course, it would be rude to say as much. Instead, I pasted a polite smile onto my face...and deflected like a pro.

"I didn't get to tell you about my job earlier," I started. "But I'll be working on campus. Baking cupcakes. Well, and other stuff too. Plus manning the coffee bar and taking out the trash. Actually, I'm supposed to start today...."

"You're babbling," Chief Greenbriar interrupted after a long moment. His nostrils flared and he cocked his head in consideration. But to my relief, the older man appeared amused rather than annoyed by the cascade of trivialities.

"Yes, sir. Sorry," I answered. "I just really, really like cupcakes."

Having run out of further blind alleys to talk us down, I held my breath, hoping the verbal detour would succeed. Unfortunately, Chief Greenbriar didn't let me off the hook so easily. Instead, he pierced me with one of those gazes that seemed to peer directly into my soul before pinning me right back down with pointed words. "You're saying you traveled all this way to work a job among *humans*?"

And there it was, the call to either lie about my brother or tell the unfortunate truth. Something in my gut said that Chief Greenbriar wouldn't be so thrilled to invite me into his pack if I let slip that I wasn't simply a mating-age female hunting for a new pack to call home. But would I be putting my brother at risk by bringing his presence into the limelight?

With no better option on the table, I accepted the inevitable and told the truth. "No, sir. This has nothing to do with humans," I admitted, ignoring the vivid mental image of dark hair falling across equally dark eyes that impinged for a brief instant upon my internal landscape. Shaking my head ever so slightly to remove Sebastien's face from view, I elaborated. "I'm here hunting for Derek...."

Then I winced, realizing I lacked a surname to tack onto that threadbare explanation. For all I knew, the *first* name I'd been using wasn't even the right one. Because my brother had initially introduced himself online as Roadrunner, and he'd equivocated for quite some time before offering any additional information beyond that. Who was to say "Derek" hadn't been lying, at least by omission, when he finally coughed up a real name?

And who was to say—given my previous lack of contact with biological family—that Derek was even my brother at all?

None of my internal confusion was lost upon Chief Greenbriar, who placed a fatherly hand atop my bowed shoulder. "If you don't even know this male's last name, perhaps he's not worth searching for," he told me kindly. "My son, on the other hand, has a pedigree that traces back to the Mayflower. In twenty years, he'll be alpha in my place...and you could be that alpha's mate."

I could have argued that I'd never been told this heir apparent's *first* name, which definitely put him a step below Derek on the know-o-meter. Still, that wasn't the point.

Instead, I spent a moment assuming the demeanor of strawberry shortcake, all fluffy and sweet with vanilla-flavored whipped cream on top. Then I tilted my head to emphasize our height difference before playing my trump card. "I think I gave you the wrong impression, sir. I'm not here to find a life partner. I'm hunting for my *brother.*"

"Ah."

Chief Greenbriar's self-satisfied smirk relaxed my shoulders for the first time since I'd woken up alone on the cold, hard ground. My temporary alpha hadn't been thrilled at the idea of me spouse-hunting outside his nuclear family, but I felt as clearly as if he'd spoken that he was quite willing to let me stay on in order to track down an elusive sibling. After all, what better way to trick a non-pack female into partnering with his son than to keep me close at hand where I could be easily managed?

Sure enough, when the alpha spoke again, it was to lay out ground rules I was easily able to accept. Well, not the first one—I lied and told my host that I already had a place to stay when he tried to offer up his guest room for my accommodations. But I willingly agreed to dine with the Greenbriar family every evening...despite the sinking suspicion that a single mating-aged son would be the only shifter to show up at the event, turning what should have been a pack affair into a de facto date.

"I appreciate your hospitality," I told Chief Greenbriar rather than arguing the point. These rules I could live with, and I was glad to have been let off the hook so easily.

But my temporary alpha continued speaking, talking over me as if I hadn't even opened my mouth. "And on the seventh day, you and Aaron will make your mating bond official. It will be my pleasure to welcome you as my daughter-in-law and as the newest member of the Greenbriar pack."

Well, at least now I knew my supposed fiancé's name. It was a start, right?

Chapter 8

The dawn meeting with Chief Greenbriar took the wind out of my sails so thoroughly that I slumped atop my suitcase for ten solid minutes before remembering I had places to go and people to see. But first, I pulled out my phone and paged back through missed calls. *Dad, Dad, Dad, Mom, Dad, a cousin, an aunt, an uncle, Dad, Dad, Dad, Dad.*

At least I wouldn't have to flounder around trying to decide who should be contacted first. The frequency of Wolfie's calls suggested he was a hair's breadth away from worried-parent meltdown. Time to pull out the big guns and remove my father figure from the hunt.

To that end, I spent another minute unzipping my suitcase and rifling through my possessions in search of the small plastic container that held my own personal party favor. And when I popped open the lid to the single-serving cupcake box, my throat tightened with homesickness so abrupt it nearly sent me scurrying back to the nearest bus station with my tail between my legs.

Because I'd half expected to be sent on my way with a joke cake, maybe something built out of doggie bones to remind me to trust my lupine instincts. I'd been ready to take my father to task if he dressed up the icing in my least favorite color—orange—or ruined the sugary concoction by imbuing it with a yucky licorice flavor.

Instead, Dad must have spent long hours with frosting bag in hand in order to craft the work of art that currently sat atop my pastry. The scene was as elaborate as that found on the highest class wedding cake despite its diminutive size.

Haven—my home—sat upon a field of chocolate, small houses interspersed with wolves and humans built from spun sugar seasoned with carefully applied food coloring. I could pick out individuals easily, not just based on their location across the landscape, but from their stances and actions as well.

Next door to Wolfie's and Terra's home, my gardening aunts were busy tending roses that spiraled up the face of my own small cottage. Meanwhile, my car-loving uncle scrubbed his Ferrari while two pups frolicked in the spray of water that was supposed to be washing down the sleek black hood.

Off to one side stood my parents, Dad in lupine form and Mom human with one loving hand resting atop her mate's furry head. Their customary pose showcased more than two decades of shared affection, and I could almost smell their signature aromas as I leaned in for a closer look.

That was just the window-dressing, though. The clear purpose of this cupcake message lay in the exact center of the village green: a tremendous yellow flower that didn't actually exist. Well, the plant wasn't literally present in our community gathering space...but metaphorically I knew at a glance that the floral monster referred to me.

Because "Buttercup" had been my father's pet name for me ever since I was a child. And the plant was not only physically central to the scene, every eye was riveted upon its glowing yellow expanse.

The cupcake meant love...and Dad knew I'd be unable to eat the dessert without picking up the phone and giving him a call. So I pressed his name on the screen with one sticky finger even as I licked a cousin off the edge of the frosted panorama. This particular teenager tasted like oranges and cinnamon—his signature aroma perfectly replicated in sugary splendor. Exactly how long had Dad spent crafting this offering to have imbued such loving detail into every aspect of the scene?

"I'm eating my cupcake," I croaked around a mouthful of frosting and tears as soon as the click on the other end of the line indicated my call had gone through. And while a human father would have been torn apart by the emotion so vividly apparent in my voice, Wolfie merely hummed his approval with the smugness of a wolf.

"Then I guess we can turn around," Dad growled, his voice just barely human. And I couldn't prevent the short bark of laughter as I realized Wolfie really *had* jumped into the car as soon as the Greenbriar mantle obscured his usual ability to tap into my mental state.

Wait a minute. He wasn't.... "You're *driving*?" I demanded, imagining the four-car pileups that would result when Wolfie decided to slide around corners at his inner beast's behest....while completely disregarding all human rules of the road. Preventing my father from driving was one of the pack's most closely adhered to tenets. What had they been thinking to give him access to the keys?

"Relax." This was Mom's voice, fainter but still easily under-standable despite the phone's tinny speaker. "I'm the one be-hind the wheel. And I'm pulling over...right...now."

Only when Terra spoke did I notice that there was a second item at the bottom of the box where the cupcake had recently sat. Once again, my throat tightened as I recognized the small rectangular card, worn and tattered from the endless games she and I had played during my three-year-long Monopoly obses-sion.

"A get-out-of-jail free card?" I asked, words ungainly as I took another bite out of the frosted adornments, this time chomping down on my uncle's beloved car. Luckily, the ma-chine tasted like lemon rather than gasoline or oil—a sly nod to the fact that Chase's vehicle had cost so much to bring back up to speed that he might as well have bought it brand spank-ing new.

"Just in case you need the help," Mom answered. "Not that I think you will."

Then all three of us lapsed into companionable silence as I ate my way through the rest of my relatives and their most precious possessions. Dad had been more poetic than literal in several instances...which meant the entire cupcake turned into a medley of deliciousness rather than harboring hints of swamp muck and leaf mold. And by the time I'd eaten down to the fluffy cake interior—and discovered a molten truffle core—I could feel the strength of dozens of beloved werewolves buoy-ing me up despite the borrowed mantle that cut off our direct mental connection.

"I have to be at work in two hours," I told my parents at last rather than explaining why I'd taken so long to call...and that I was now promised to an alpha's son if I didn't track down my brother and beat it out of town within the next six and a half days.

Usually, Dad would have sensed my conflicted emotions down the pack bond. He would have nibbled away at my resistance until I admitted that I'd woken that morning with the deep-seated urge to run home to Haven with my tail between my legs. Slowly, he would have drawn me out until I admitted that I'd been badly shaken by Chief Greenbriar's ogle and subsequent ultimatum. And then my father would have done everything in his power to make those problems go away.

But today, the borrowed mantle eliminated our usual close connection, so all Wolfie had to go on was the sound of my voice on the other end of the phone. He could hear me inhale deeply, but he couldn't understand that with each lungful of air came the deep realization that I was risking the family I adored more than anything in the hopes of finding a brother who might not want to be found. Wolfie heard me exhale, but didn't feel my gut-deep acceptance of the risk I was accepting for the sake of a sibling who'd never even told me his own last name.

"I love you," I said at last, rather than trying to use words to explain what Dad and I usually communicated with raw emotion and short grunts.

"We love you too, Buttercup," Wolfie replied. And for a split second, I could feel him encircling me with those strong, familiar arms despite the Greenbriar bond that dulled the contact with my true pack. I closed my eyes and stretched my mind as far as it would go until everyone was there around me for one split second—Mom and Dad and uncles and aunts and cousins too numerous to count.

Finally, without another word, I let my lids rise and the connection fade away. Clicking off the phone, I tucked my empty cupcake wrapper back inside the waiting suitcase and rose to my feet.

I had pastries to bake and a brother to find. Only then could I return to Haven and take my proper place within the pack.

Chapter 9

After dragging a heavy suitcase across several miles of bumpy terrain during my return to civilization, I was huffing and puffing and running a bit behind. But my wolf gnawed at my stomach, angling us away from campus and toward a different neighborhood entirely. And since I was just as worried about Harmony as my animal half was, I chose an indirect route toward my ultimate destination, disembarking from the train in a poorer section of town than the one that college students usually frequented.

Human muggers weren't the reason a growl rose from my throat, though, as I stepped up to the soot-streaked wall surrounding Harmony's apartment complex. No, I found myself clenching my fists and fighting for control for a different reason entirely. The door smelled like wolf.

Instantly, my formerly somnolent animal half rose up behind my eyes, nearly ripping control out of my human hands with the intensity of her reaction to perceived danger. And with the beast at the fore, scents grew so intense that I was forced to stop stock still, only vaguely aware that I was blocking the flow of traffic while gazing intently at the building's front door.

Together, my wolf and I assessed the barrier. A hefty lock promised to guard against unauthorized admittance. But any

Tom, Dick, or Harry could currently walk right on through since a length of wood had been wedged between the door and frame to keep the portal from falling all the way shut.

An even louder growl ripped itself from my human throat. And as my lips parted to allow the sound out, the scent of shifter slammed its way in. Fox musk and fur. Lust and the urge to mate. The rapist had been here. This morning...but also yesterday afternoon and the night before and the day before that. He'd walked through this opening dozens of times, had done who knew what to Harmony while I'd slept off my elk dinner in the national forest the night before.

The fox-scented shifter had harmed someone who was *mine*. Now I would find him and tear him apart.

Then a human shoulder slammed into my side, knocking me out of the path of foot traffic and reminding me that I was supposed to be squashing my lupine nature while surrounded by innocent one-bodies. Accepting that nudge for the impetus it was, I followed my nose up the stairs and down a narrow hallway before sliding to a halt in front of a banged-up wooden door.

I could smell the rapist here just as clearly as I'd sensed him outside. He'd stood in this exact same spot mere hours earlier, sniffing at the crack just like I was currently doing. He'd waited on Harmony to emerge from her protected lair. And...then what? Had the stalker finished the job begun earlier in the evening? Had he assaulted the woman my own inner wolf had chosen as part of our pack?

I shook my head to clear it both of rage and of less familiar emotions that currently ricocheted through my body and brain. My wolf was urging me to draw this human into our inner circle, to bare our teeth and protect her with our life. But that instinct, while gospel to my lupine nature, made no rational sense to my human brain.

Because, sure, it was my responsibility to prevent Harmony—and any other innocent human—from falling afoul of shifter power struggles. But the female in question wasn't a wolf and she wasn't part of my pack. As such, the proper way to protect an unwitting one-body was to go up the chain of command and let Chief Greenbriar deal with the issue as he saw fit.

Tonight, I promised my wolf. I'd talk to the local alpha at dinner and ask him to place Harmony under his protection. In the meantime, the best option was to walk away so my presence wouldn't draw additional werewolf attention to this human's battered door.

I hadn't quite managed to talk my feet into motion, though, before the portal swung open to reveal the woman my wolf and I had gone to such lengths to track down. Harmony was far less coiffed than previously, a food-splattered sleep shirt barely hiding her curves while a wriggling toddler bounced on her left hip. But despite the domesticity of their pose, two sets of dark eyes widened as one when they took in the presence of a predator waiting in the hall.

BERATING MYSELF FOR allowing wolfishness to terrorize the innocent, I struggled to tamp down my inner animal post haste. But before my lupine half was even partially subdued, the child began babbling out a welcome that meant nothing to my human ears yet said "Oh boy!" and "Hello!" and "Play with me!" to my wolf.

For her part, Harmony's greeting emerged a mere hair's breadth behind. "Come on in," the woman told me, opening the door wider and motioning me inside. Despite her initial emotional reaction, the human clearly recognized me from the previous evening and appeared abundantly willing to give me benefit of the doubt.

Not smart, my human brain decided.

Still, feet carried me forward on the wind of wolf instinct even as my rational brain rebelled against entering Harmony's domain. I really hadn't intended to do anything beyond reassuring myself that my current companion had bounced back from last night's trauma. But the child's eyes drew me closer step by step until my finger trailed across feather-soft wisps of fur atop her tender infant skull. And I softened yet further as the youngster's fingers curled gently around my outstretched thumb.

To my surprise, Harmony didn't swipe her offspring out from under my nose the way I would have expected. Instead, the other female glanced down at my suitcase then up at my matted hair with narrowed eyes. Finally, closing the door behind my back, she slid the safety chain into place and locked us all inside. "You spent the night on the streets," she said.

A human would have sidestepped the issue, would have danced the polka of politeness until the woman before us let the issue drop. But I wasn't human. And I'd realized as soon as the pup's tiny fingers touched my skin that I wasn't leaving this family undefended.

Because why relinquish Harmony into Chief Greenbriar's dubious care when I could protect her the easy way, by staking my own claim hard and fast? If that meant making the other female think I was homeless so she'd invite me to spend the night...well, that would be easy since I technically had no other place to stay.

Ours, my wolf reiterated simply, and this time we were in full agreement. I'd move in and scent mark every inch of this building until any shifter in his right mind gave the residence a wide berth. Eventually, we'd find Derek and be forced to make other arrangements. But for now, these humans were ours to protect.

To that end, I smiled shyly and agreed with Harmony's assessment. "I'm looking for a room to rent," I told the mother boldly while wiggling my ears to entertain her offspring. The latter descended into a chorus of musical giggles, proving that wolf pups and human pups weren't so different after all.

Another string of babble emerged from the little girl's lips, then she was flinging herself through the air between us, landing in my waiting arms as ably as any monkey. And as the child's warmth soaked through the intervening t-shirt, I could have sworn infantile heat made its way through my skin and impacted the heart underneath.

"You are a charmer," I whispered, lowering my head to nibble ever so gently upon the lobe of one tiny ear. The toddler smelled like innocence, joy, and sunshine. Tastier than a cupcake, more tantalizing than any bar of European chocolate. I wanted to shift into lupine form and snuggle the little critter until she fell asleep cradled between four furry paws.

And while I would have expected Harmony to swipe the child back, my hostess instead stuck to business. "How long will you be in town?" the other woman asked, seemingly unconcerned by her daughter's traitorous jump into a stranger's waiting arms.

"Six nights," I answered quickly. No way was I planning to remain behind once Chief Greenbriar's clock ticked down to marriage-ville. And if I was forced to leave earlier...well, from the looks of Harmony's scrupulously clean but seriously shabby furnishings, my hostess could use the extra cash.

The time frame seemed to be acceptable to all involved. "For a week, I can move into Mama's room and give you my bed," Harmony began.

Only, before my companion could name a price, the sound of a cane tapping across linoleum put our incipient deal on pause. The newcomer who appeared around the corner was wizened with age, a bent back and a preponderance of wrinkles giving me the impression of a fragile elder who should be cosseted and protected.

But the matriarch's eyes were even darker and more piercing than her daughter's. And her head whipped from side to side with the speed of a power mixer. "No," she told Harmony before erupting into a stream of Spanish far too rapid for me to follow.

I did catch one word, though. *Bruja*. Harmony's mother was calling me a witch.

Chapter 10

"**M**ama," Harmony protested. Still, she plucked the toddler back out of my arms as adroitly as ever a mother bear stepped between a pack of dangerous werewolves and her curious yet innocent offspring. "We aren't *campesinas supersticiosas*. Speak English so our guest can understand."

I forced a healthy helping of confusion onto my face even though my own grasp of Spanish was good enough to know that Harmony was accusing her mother of being a superstitious peasant. Unfortunately for me, the older woman's subsequent words were even easier to understand.

"You. Leave," the matriarch ordered, pointing at the door behind my back with all the force of a parent chasing a stray dog out of her spotless kitchen. Meanwhile, the older woman's grip slid down the shaft of the cane as if she fully intended to use the weapon to protect herself...or perhaps to club me to death.

And no wonder. As I edged around Harmony and neared the diminutive yet powerful elder, I caught a hint of fox musk clinging to her weapon. Had the old woman risen in the night, seen a werewolf at the door, and chased him away with her trusty stick? Did something about my own posture reveal the lupine nature hidden beneath my human skin?

Sensitive one-bodies often reacted negatively to alpha werewolves like myself, which was part of the reason why I'd brought so many cupcakes along on my road trip. Unfortunately, I was completely out of sugary bribes at the moment. Instead, I donned my most sincere smile and attacked with an honorific combined with pure honesty.

"*Doña,* I'm not here to harm your daughter and granddaughter," I told the older woman, raising my hands as if their emptiness would prove I was neither witch nor wolf. "I'm just looking for a place to spend a few nights. Nothing more, I promise."

In response, the grandmother's nostrils flared and her eyes flashed. I could tell that she'd noticed my lapse, had tuned into the way I'd skipped right over the human promise to leave if I wasn't welcome. The trouble was, I knew I wasn't welcome...and I still wasn't leaving.

Well, not for another hour and fifteen minutes, at which point I needed to be on campus and ready to start my first shift at the coffee shop.

Taking a deep breath, I tried to figure out how to change a mind that appeared as stubbornly made up as my own. But Harmony solved the problem for me. "Mama, this is ludicrous," the younger woman said, stepping in front of her mother's cane without worrying that the stick might come down upon her unprotected back. "Ember is a friend and she's staying here this week whether you like it or not."

The old woman didn't buy her daughter's reassurance, I could tell. Instead, she and I locked gazes in a stare every bit as intense as a werewolf challenge of wills.

But, in the end, my opponent gave in. Shaking her head angrily, she turned away and stomp-tapped back down the hallway. She wasn't happy...but apparently Harmony was alpha in this household despite the latter's relatively tender age.

I'd definitely need to mend that bridge in the future, but there was nothing I could do about the old woman's dislike now. On the other hand.... "Blueberry muffins?" I whispered to Harmony, hoping old ears weren't werewolf-sharp.

"Her favorite," the younger woman agreed.

LEAVING MY SUITCASE behind in the hands of a human family who already felt strangely like pack, I hightailed it back toward the subway station and boarded a train bound for campus. And in that moment of enforced stillness while the vehicle conveyed me toward the college, I pulled the chain out from beneath my shirt and considered my brother's hidden key.

The number "*404*" was engraved in the center, ringed by a smaller admonition: "*Do not duplicate.*" But there was no explanation, leaving me with more questions than answers.

Did the key belong to a room? To a safe-deposit box? To a padlock? I wasn't sure...and I didn't have time to worry the issue further because I needed to switch lines and clock in at my new job ASAP.

Still, I nibbled around the edges of the enigma while racing across a summer-empty walkway in order to catch up with the cafeteria manager who'd offered me this gig. And I worried the problem up and down while collecting a pass card that allowed me to open the doors of my newfound shop.

And, okay, I'll admit that I lost track of the mystery for several long minutes while relaxing into the wonder of having a commercial kitchen at my beck and call. There were brownies to bake, frozen blueberries to retrieve from the pantry in preparation for creating a batch of muffins bound to sweeten the sour temperament of Harmony's elderly mother. After that....

"Are you open?"

The jingle of a bell combined with a timid voice caught my attention as the first customers of the day blew in from outside. The two females were evidently students...perhaps friends of Derek's? And while I served them with a smile, I also nudged my smartphone a little further down the counter, brushing my fingers across the darkened screen to bring Derek's unsmiling face eye-catchingly to life.

It was time to remember my larger goal and lure in some confidences out of the wild.

Unfortunately, the gaze of the shorter girl skittered over my brother as if he didn't exist. The other customer's pupils, though, dilated with interest. "Do you know him?" I asked innocently, gesturing toward Derek's handsome face while handing over a paper cup full of steaming liquid.

"Your boyfriend?" the second student answered. "Naw, but he's a hottie."

And, just as quickly as I'd thought her hooked, I cranked in my reel to find bait gone and line empty. "See you tomorrow," I told the two with a nearly inaudible sigh, not bothering to correct the student's assumption about Derek's and my relationship. Then I forced my feet to dance with their previous joy as I returned to the oven, casting off the leaden weights that had threatened to materialize at the ends of my formerly buoyant feet.

"Of course it won't be that easy. I don't even know if Derek went to school here," I reminded myself, my voice echoing oddly in the empty space as I got back to work creating treats so tantalizing they'd draw just the right sort of prey in my door. There were plenty of people on this campus beyond the students. Perhaps Derek had cleaned the floors or merely wandered along the walkways enjoying the scenery. Whatever his reason for mentioning the spot during our video chats, I was confident that some person with information pertaining to my brother's current whereabouts would eventually drop by. I just needed to settle in and wait....

To that end, I whipped up a batch of triple-chocolate cupcakes, decorating the domed tops with artful curls of yet more chocolate along with a thin drizzle of raspberry syrup. Those were immediate crowd pleasers, so I branched out into another confection...this time concocting a chocolate croissant intended to gratify the supposed fiancé I'd meet for the first time in human form tonight.

After that, business picked up to the point where I no longer had time for baking. Instead, I busied myself changing customers' minds about what they thought they wanted. First, I tempted an elderly professor into choosing the brownies over the muffin he thought would please his health-conscious wife, then I actually managed to bring a smile to a scowling student's lips as she nibbled around the edges of a tartlet filled with rich, sweet blueberry jam.

And yet, every time I nudged my phone to life and drew human eyes to my brother's image, a sublime lack of awareness remained on my customer's faces. Meanwhile, with every moment that passed, Chief Greenbriar's deadline hung heavier upon my slender shoulders.

Had Derek just been teasing me with his frequent mentions of this tree-lined campus? Or perhaps my brother had been trying to impress by referring to an institution that possessed sufficient name recognition for its prestige to carry over into the werewolf world.

By four hours into my shift, I was hovering on the edge of quitting the job I'd only just begun. Because I was tying up half of every day in a coffee shop when I could have been out pounding the pavement and sniffing for any sign of my brother's scent throughout the city. Perhaps it was time to be honest and admit that I'd applied for this position not because of Derek's dropped hints but instead due to a selfish urge to surround myself with baked goods during my first solo adventure away from my home pack.

Before I could tease apart my own ulterior motives, though, breath caught in my throat. The brownie-eating professor had slipped out the door while I pondered further options, and in the process a tendril of outside air blew inside in the older man's wake. The hint of aroma flooding my workspace shouldn't have been out of place on a college campus...yet, it still froze me in place just as thoroughly as the scent trail of an elk had done the night before.

The air was filled with the tang of dusty old books. Scintillating sandalwood. And heart-pounding adventure.

Forcing reluctant muscles to flex while slowing my breathing with an effort, I lifted my chin to take in the scene beyond the window...and my gaze instantly locked with dark orbs as familiar as my own. Sebastien—my Uber driver—was peering through the plate-glass and directly into my soul.

Chapter 11

For fifteen interminable seconds, my body rebelled against explicit instructions to stay calm, cool, and collected. My chest heaved, my cheeks reddened, and I panted like a sprinter stuck at mile five of a marathon as I attempted to wrap my mind around the vision outside my shop. Had Sebastien really been this handsome when I ran into him the previous night?

Struggling to breathe against the vise-like pressure in my chest, I found myself tracing the human's outline with hungry eyes. Sunlight glinted against jet-black hair and the lines of Sebastien's jaw were so sharp that my hand rose without permission in an effort to stroke his stubbled chin. The human's chest was as broad as any werewolf's, his stance calm and confident. But it was his eyes that snagged my attention and drew me in further yet.

There were mysteries hidden within those dark depths. A flicker of pain, a hint of regret. Mostly, though, the newcomer's face told me what I desperately wanted to hear—that Sebastien considered me every bit as enticing as I found him.

The muffled tinkle of the bell above the door broke through my reverie, then hard-soled shoes rang out across intervening tiles. "Is it too late to snag a coffee?" Sebastien asked, gaze rising to the clock above my head before his eyes pierced mine once more.

The cafe was supposed to close in five minutes, but I busied my hands filling a cup anyway. Better working than reaching out and pulling this human close enough to sniff the tantalizing aroma emanating from the crook of his neck....

"Were you delivering somebody to campus this afternoon?" I asked, interrupting thoughts that I couldn't afford to have flow any further. Glancing over one shoulder, I was proud of the fact that my voice remained steady despite my heart continuing to beat a staccato in my chest.

Unfortunately, I was paying more attention to Sebastien's anticipated answer than to the hot liquid nearing the top of the cup. Because just as an expression I didn't entirely understand wafted across Sebastien's chiseled countenance, coffee overflowed across my fingers, stinging tender flesh.

"Ow!" I exclaimed, barely managing to take four steps to the sink before the cup slipped and spilled across the stainless-steel expanse. *So much for coffee.*

Then Sebastien was there beside me. The fabric of his sports coat brushed against my arm and his scent enfolded me as the male reached across my body to turn on the cold-water tap. Before I knew what was happening, warm fingers were nudging my wound beneath the soothing flow, human contact doing more than icy water to dull my pain.

I could have stood like that for hours, soaking up Sebastien's intoxicating aroma like the scent of a baking cake. But the coffee hadn't been quite hot enough to truly burn. And if I let this go on for much longer, my wolf was going to take the lead and do something we'd later regret.

We won't regret anything, my inner animal murmured even as I slipped out from beneath Sebastien's arm and took two long steps back.

"Thanks," I said to my human companion, ignoring the complaints of my inner wolf. "I really appreciate the help. But health-department regulations require all customers to remain on the other side of the counter...."

My words flew fast and furious, building a wall between us. And, in response, my companion raised one dark brow quizzically before proceeding to obey. Footsteps against tile, the whoosh of moving air, then my companion was safely back in the seating area from which he'd come.

"Better?" he asked, elbows leaning against the scratched counter.

And I nodded...even though my affirmative was a total lie.

THIS TIME AROUND, I was more careful as I filled a cup with steaming liquid. And Sebastien followed my lead, retreating to surface pleasantries as I finished up my work.

"The Uber thing is just a side gig," my customer said, returning to my original question at long last. And as he spoke, he pulled out a credit card and a rectangle of card stock to exchange for his cup of joe.

"Sebastien Carter, Professor of Psychology," the business card read, along with a phone number and email address.

Huh. Now *that* was interesting. What college professor willingly chose to spend his evenings shuttling random strangers from point A to point B? And what perspicacious werewolf would have missed the fact that her driver's sports car was far too fancy to be used for ten-dollar taxi fares?

Kicking my ailing brain back into gear, I leapt to conclusions I should have drawn hours ago. "You're a student of human nature," I guessed. "You signed up with Uber so you could observe people in their element."

"Guilty as charged," Sebastien answered, eyes crinkling up at the corners as his face broke out into a breathtaking smile. Yet again, I found my chest tightening as I struggled to inhale.

In an effort to regain proper focus, I bent down to examine the nearly empty display of pastries, trying to decide which selection would suit my current customer the best. Last night, Sebastien had chosen the chocolate...a decadent and seductive move hinting at enigmatic depths beneath his apparently cleancut persona.

But the choices at the time had been severely limited and the current cocoa-related option—triple chocolate chunk—was a whole 'nother ball game of complexities. Would Sebastien prefer one of the milk-chocolate oatmeal cookies I'd stirred up after realizing that most of my customers were searching for fiber along with their jolt of sweet? Or perhaps....

"That one."

Ah, so he was a decider. I liked that in a customer. No hovering indecisively above the most tasty choice while calculating future impact to heart and liver. No wishy-washy meanderings down the candy aisle, tasting each treat with hungry eyes before allowing a single morsel to touch his lips. No, Sebastien saw what he wanted...and he took it.

What would it feel like if the thing he wanted had been *me*?

Shivering, I raised my eyes from the display case and found Sebastien squatting with his head on the exact same level as my own. A thick sheet of glass and several feet of air separated us, but I could almost feel the professor's pointer finger trailing across my lips, around one ear, then down along the side of my jaw. For the first time in my life, in fact, I experienced a sensation more enticing than the first taste of 70% chocolate...and Sebastien hadn't even touched his finger to my bare skin.

"The triple-chocolate cupcake," my customer elaborated when I remained frozen and tongue-tied. "I like...the curls."

Tendrils of my own hair had escaped from its health-department-approved bun while I worked, and now a wisp brushed against my face in counterpoint to Sebastien's statement. The cheek in question heated up yet again and I knew my blush would be bright red and obvious—embarrassing when faced with nothing more than a little innocent flirting.

Turning away to hide my reaction, I managed to grab the most elaborately decorated cupcake...and the one to which my customer's finger had seemed unerringly drawn. "It isn't too froufrou?" I murmured, my voice catching on the final word.

"I'm a connoisseur of beauty," Sebastien said softly as the first hint of fur—a response to his presence—broke out along my spine.

And then my companion reached forward to accept the chocolate treat, our fingers brushing as paper-coated pastry transferred from hand to hand. Only as sparks of profound awareness ran from fingertips all the way down my spine did I realize that I'd meant to put the pastry in a box with a couple of napkins, to follow the health-code rules to the letter.

Yet another violation—I was seriously flubbing my job as barista today. And yet, I found that I didn't care about the lapse one bit.

My wolf didn't mind the oversight either. Instead, she pressed against the inside of my skin, hunting for a way to come out and join in the fun. *Shhh, not now,* I told my inner animal. But I pressed my lips closely together rather than continuing our banter, afraid of what my companion would see if I opened my mouth to speak.

After all, fur came first, but the next symptom of an incipient shift was generally fangs. Not quite what this innocent human was expecting to have delivered along with his cupcake.

Sebastien, darn him, seemed entirely unaffected by the same skin-on-skin contact that had sent me reeling. "I don't just study human nature in the wild, you know," he continued, carefully peeling back the paper from each dark-chocolate ridge of the treat in his hand. The professor paused as a segment of pastry caught on the lining, and after backing off the pressure he tried again from a different angle. This time the wrapper came away clean.

"Hmm?" I answered, not hearing a single word Sebastien had to say. Because I'd gotten lost in another flight of fancy, this time wondering what it would feel like to have that same attention applied to the buttons of my shirt, the zipper of my pants, the skin along the side of my neck....

"The business card," my companion reminded me, gesturing toward the pale rectangle that lay abandoned atop the nearby counter. "I'm running experiments this summer on campus. They're easy and fun. Each session takes about an hour and pays ten bucks plus a candy bar. It's the candy that draws the students in."

He smiled again, a devastating widening of lush lips that sent my stomach plummeting down toward the sticky floor. That expression on Sebastien's face should be *outlawed*. It was definitely contrary to the purpose of the health code—keeping me alive long enough to finish out my shift.

"I hope you'll come by and give it a try," the professor continued. "Maybe tomorrow?"

I think I might have nodded, although I can't be entirely certain. Instead, I watched as the pastry I'd baked with my own two hands rose toward Sebastien's lips. The experience was a close second cousin to being kissed, especially when warm breath flung the scent of chocolate and coffee out of Sebastien's mouth and toward my flaring nostrils....

Then the bell above the door rang yet again and the moment was broken. Letting the uneaten cupcake drift down to his side, Sebastien swiveled around and watched with raised eyebrows as two very angry werewolves pushed their way through the open door.

Chapter 12

"What do you think you're doing?" the fox-scented shifter demanded. I recognized him immediately, not from any glimpse of a face that I might have caught in the dark alley the night before, but because he looked precisely the way he smelled. In human form, the male was tall and lanky, his angular countenance made even more rat-like by its squinty-eyed expression of distaste. Harmony's potential rapist was definitely the last person I'd hoped to see that day.

But before I could usher the male out of my shop, a second voice rang out across the room. "Roger," this one warned.

The second werewolf to speak was more appealing...especially once the alpha's son reached up to place a steadying hand atop his underling's shoulder. Like his companion, I recognized Aaron by scent, and I was vaguely aware that I should have been spending this time assessing my supposed fiancé as mate material. Instead, I found myself more interested in the way the heir apparent's touch so effectively reduced the angry energy of his companion down to a dull roar. Apparently Aaron shared alpha capabilities with his powerful father.

The pack leader's son also possessed the familial ability to exude geniality on command. Stepping forward, he offered a hand to Sebastien while producing a one-body-friendly smile. "Aaron Greenbriar, a friend of Ember's."

"Sebastien Carter, ditto."

I was warmed by Sebastien's claimed friendship. But then I winced as the cupcake—which had been juggled from hand to hand in preparation for the human-style greeting—slipped out of the professor's grip. He grabbed for the falling pastry, barely missed its descent, then watched in dismay as the offering landed icing down on the scuffed and dirty floor.

Sweaty skin, hot kisses, and other entirely imaginary aspects of the preceding moments instantly dissipated into grime and disillusionment. And Sebastien evidently shared my chagrin because he released a stream of syllables that I suspected was invective in...maybe Swahili?

I wanted to bask in this evidence that my attraction hadn't been entirely one-sided. But Aaron's shoulders were tense and rat-faced Roger's laugh seemed intended to start a fight that no human could ever win. So I palmed both my phone and Sebastien's card as surreptitiously as possible, then glanced at the clock to support my upcoming lie.

"I'm sorry," I said, "But I've gotta shut things down. The door locks automatically fifteen minutes after closing and I definitely don't want to spend the night sleeping on icing-covered floors. So I'm afraid I can't sell you another cupcake today...."

Never mind that there were three similar chocolate confections remaining in the case along with several other types of dessert, all of which would be good for nothing but the dumpster come morning. I'd be handing out leftovers to all and sundry after work...but I couldn't afford to let Sebastien spend one more moment in the danger zone. "See you later," I continued, my eyes adding: *Why won't you go already?*

And Sebastien moved...but he didn't obey. Instead, side-stepping two burly werewolves, the professor stepped closer to the counter until the two of us stood nose to nose, surroundings hidden by the proximity of the other's face. "I'll see you tomorrow," he offered far too quietly for Aaron and Roger to hear...

...Well, too quietly for them to hear if they'd been human.

Unfortunately, the two bystanders weren't precisely human and they picked up the professor's words far too well. "Should we put the chairs up on the tables?" Aaron suggested loudly, as if he'd been helping close cafes all his life. Playing along, Roger added: "Where's the broom?"

Tuning out my pesky chaperones, I scooted one hand a fraction of a centimeter further across the cool glass countertop. I wasn't accustomed to human mating rituals, wasn't accustomed to the impulse to gauge every move carefully so I'd both capture Sebastien's attention while also allowing myself to save face when and if my interest wasn't reciprocated.

Only, Sebastien didn't ignore my advancing fingers. Instead, his larger hand slipped beneath mine, our joined appendages rising as a unit until his lips could brush butterfly-soft kisses across my sensitive skin. Behind his back someone—I thought it was Roger—began to growl just barely low enough to elude the professor's ears.

I was playing with fire and I knew it. Still, Sebastien's kiss curled the corners of my mouth up into a smile while my other hand fingered the corners of the business card now buried deep within my front pants pocket. "Tomorrow," I agreed.

Then, before either Aaron or Roger could chase down the human rapidly retreating across the tile floor, I shot out orders with my best alpha oomph to back them up. "The broom is in the closet behind your back, Roger. And, yes, Aaron, we'll be out of here twice as quickly if you put up the chairs."

WHEN SEBASTIEN WAS present, the air had been so full of testosterone that I might as well have possessed two jealous fake-fiancés rather than just one. But the instant the human turned the corner and disappeared from sight, the act—and the broom handle Roger had been holding awkwardly in his arms—clattered to the floor.

"This *thing* my father thinks he's orchestrating," Aaron began, waving a hand between the two of us, "isn't going to happen."

The shifter's jaw worked furiously as he prepared to dive into a long-winded explanation that likely ended with, *"It's not me, it's you."* But I beat him to the punch. "Agreed," I said simply.

"What you have to understand..." Aaron continued, then broke off as he realized I hadn't offered up a single argument. And, predictably, alpha werewolfishness rose up behind my companion's eyes at the perceived slight.

Because, sure, Aaron had wanted to ditch me first. But I'd been the one shooting him down in the end...and that just wasn't kosher. "Look," the male started, advancing toward me angrily.

This time it was Roger who placed a chastising hand on the shorter male's shoulder, and my eyebrows rose at the abrupt change of roles. Rather than remarking upon the inconsistency, though, I gave the alpha's son an easy out.

"Under other circumstances, I'd be honored to become your mate," I jumped in quickly, trying to make my voice sound honest despite the shiver of repulsion that raced up my spine at the very idea of mating with the Greenbriar heir apparent and leaving my own pack behind. "But that's not why I'm here. I'm in town for one reason and one reason alone. To hunt for my brother. Then I'm going home to my own pack where I belong. So, you see, choosing a mate isn't in the cards...at least, not right now."

And even though I'd been eying Sebastien avariciously ever since the latter crossed my path—making the preceding speech a total lie—the alpha's son accepted my explanation as gospel. "Well, that's good then," Aaron countered. "Because I can't come to dinner tonight. That's actually why I dropped by."

Now it was my turn to flinch. Chief Greenbriar wasn't going to take that particular news flash well at all, and it looked like I'd been signed up as the bearer of bad tidings. I just hoped the city's pack leader wasn't the type to shoot the messenger....

But while I remained profoundly concerned about the future—or rather, about whether I'd *get* a future—Aaron had apparently dropped all cares as soon as he got his own way. His eyes roamed greedily across the glass-fronted display case, and I sighed as I accepted the inevitable. Our meeting wouldn't be over until I rustled up some grub for my uninvited guests. After all, werewolves were always hungry and heir apparents were used to being served.

"What can I getcha?" I asked, pulling out a sheet of waxed paper to separate myself from whatever pastry Aaron might choose as his own.

Rather than responding, though, my customer wandered idly down the row, proving that he was definitely *not* a decider. And in response, I tapped my feet for ten long seconds before plucking a chocolate croissant off the tray to hurry our transaction along. I knew what my customer wanted better than he did, proven by the real pleasure that spread across Aaron's face when he inhaled the first bite.

"And for you?" I asked, tamping down disgust as I turned to rat-faced Roger. I had a feeling my final customer of the day was a licorice type of guy...mostly because a potential rapist deserved to join that detested flavor on my shit list. Of course, I didn't allow licorice in my kitchen, so I settled on a different guess in my efforts to hurry the duo out of the shop.

"I'll bet you like oatmeal cookies," I suggested with false joviality, hand already reaching to snatch the final lumpy morsel off its transparent platter. But then my brow furrowed as the second shifter's gaze instead latched onto the blueberry tartlets two trays down.

Blueberry? That selection didn't make any sense. Blueberry lovers possessed an inner core of steely integrity. And, sure, a tartlet was sweeter and less wholesome than the muffins I'd baked with Harmony's mother in mind. Still...I had a hard time lining up Roger's current choice with the man who'd pawed my landlady without permission the evening before.

But Aaron had already returned to business, leaving me no time to ponder the conundrum at length. "Can you get to Dad's house on your own?" the pack leader's son asked, speaking with his mouth full as he wolfed down his croissant like a, well, like a werewolf. If I hadn't already determined that Chief Greenbriar's son wasn't mate material, this display would have clinched the deal. After all, I preferred a little more savoring before the main event.

Then, remembering I'd been asked a question, I hastened to shrug off the male's concern. "No problem," I answered before shooing them both away from my counter. "Now, go. I really do need to finish cleaning up. Unless either of you wants to help...?"

As expected, my not-so-subtle hint was enough to send the duo scurrying for cover. And, for the first time in several hours, I was left with nothing but baked goods and the memory of Sebastien's shiver-inducing touch to keep me company.

Chapter 13

My brain hummed with questions as I jogged down the steps into the subway tunnel half an hour later...which is the only explanation I can give for why I neither smelled nor heard the mugger until his arm settled around my neck. Before I had time to retaliate, in fact, my attacker had pressed my spine up against his hard chest, giving me a good, long sniff of the aromas that should have clued me in to his presence several minutes earlier.

The stranger smelled like lust and anger and fur, the last nearly hidden beneath a human-style cologne. "This must be my lucky day," the stranger breathed, teeth lengthening into fangs as he proceeded to nibble the cartilage along the top of my ear.

I suspected the bites were my attacker's idea of foreplay. But they instead roiled my stomach and made me regret the oatmeal cookie I'd scarfed down while washing out the display cases and preparing the cafe for its nighttime rest. A teaspoonful of bile clawed its way up my throat and I opened my mouth to release odors that should have cued any sane werewolf in to my lack of interest.

But apparently my attacker wasn't sane. Instead, his whisper devolved into a nearly lupine growl as he continued spitting words and water droplets into my ear. "Imagine. A pack princess falling directly into my arms," he hummed in satisfaction. "I've landed the perfect mate."

My over-protective cousins would have told me to hit hard then run for cover. But I was more curious than afraid. Did this male really think that a little cologne to shield his scent would allow him to get away with a crime of this caliber? What was going on in this city that a friend of the alpha's son would attack a human one night and a strange shifter would go after me the next?

So I merely twisted my neck to take in my assailant's face. The male was clean-shaven, well-dressed, and looked far more like a pack werewolf than like a battered loner. Not that I recognized him from last night's hunt...but I also hadn't seen any of those shifters in human form.

"You don't look like an idiot," I said companionably while my brain raced, trying to figure out whether my favorite self-defense move would require me to drop the box of pastries I still clutched in one white-knuckled fist. I didn't particularly want to lose the blueberry muffins I'd stashed away to please my landlady's mother, but I would if I had to....

Meanwhile, I continued the attempt to return my attacker to his right mind. "You look like a smart guy without a death wish," I added. "So I can't quite figure out what you think you're doing."

Rather than answering, the male tightened his grip, cutting off all access to air. He was serious, then, not just a friend of Aaron's intent upon chasing me out of town. As if to further prove his point, the male's left hand reached across to fondle my breasts...at which point I gave up on deciphering the mystery and stomped down as hard as I could on the arch of his right foot.

The move should have worked. It would have too...had the male not been wearing such heavy boots that my attack made little impact. Without even grunting, my opponent swayed away from my flailing legs, twisting us both around until my lower limbs were clenched immobile between his hard-boned knees.

"Not so fast, vixen," he rumbled. Then, pulling upon alpha dominance that he really shouldn't have possessed, the male ordered, *"Stay."*

IN RESPONSE, I TRIED—AND failed—to shake my head in dismay. *No. This can't be happening to me.* Not since Wolfie had provided a taste of my own medicine when I was a child had I been barked into line by a stronger wolf. There just weren't many shifters out there below pack-leader status whose inner beasts were more powerful than my own.

And as I fought against the order freezing my lips and legs in place, fear clawed its way up my throat for the first time all day. *This doesn't make sense,* I growled silently, trying to keep my thoughts rational even as my wolf began whining and clawing against my insides. Why would a male so powerful he could freeze me with a single word be stalking deserted subway stations in search of an easy lay? Shouldn't my attacker be busy guiding dozens of other shifters, creating a pack of his very own instead of poaching upon someone else's?

Then reason and logic flew out the window as panic fully engulfed my inner wolf. She flung us from side to side with the force of desperation...or at least she tried to. But instead, muscles merely twitched impotently beneath our skin as the alpha compulsion held us in place as strongly as any hand.

Okay, so that's not quite true. Our struggles *did* manage to tip the cupcake box out of our fist, cardboard falling open against the concrete floor as blueberry muffins plus an array of treats intended for my Greenbriar hosts turned into so much flotsam to feed the rats.

And as quakes wracked my body while failing to move me an inch further away from my attacker, I found myself screaming silently within my own head. *I have Chief Greenbriar's permission to hunt within the city!* I told my attacker with my eyes. Then, as I grew more desperate yet: *Don't you know who my father is?*

Because it wasn't as if Wolfie's reputation was a local phenomenon. Even three states away, any shifter with a lick of sense should know that my father was bound to rip an attacker's entrails out through his nostrils if anyone dared to lay an unkind finger upon Daddy's little girl.

And yet, despite all evidence to the contrary, this male *did* very much dare to break the law. He walked around me, gaze tunneling through my clothing as a smirk filled out his weak-boned jaw. Meanwhile, the male's inner wolf rose so high behind human eyes that I wasn't entirely sure whether he wanted to rape me...or to eat me.

"Delicious," the male growled, hard fingers gripping my hips and pulling me up against his erect dick. My muscles refused to even shiver now as his head bent down to suck at the rigid tendons lining my neck.

This is really happening, I realized. Now would have been a good time to carry a canister of mace in my pocket like my landlady did...assuming frozen fingers were able to move sufficiently to deploy the physical defense, that is.

Then, before I could relinquish the final shred of hope, my attacker jolted backwards as if he'd been struck. And in the exact same instant, his cell phone chimed.

It looked like my wishful thinking had borne fruit after all. I'd been saved by the bell.

Chapter 14

T he mugger glanced at his phone's screen then took off like a shot...leaving me frozen in place with no way to break free. *Well, isn't this delightful?*

I could see it now. After doing my best to keep my nose clean, I—rather than the males who seemed to be ignoring shifter laws right and left—would be the one tossed out of the city on my ear. Or worse.

After all, human travelers would flood the station as soon as the next train arrived. I'd remain locked in place as travelers dashed from train to stairs. Most probably wouldn't even notice the oddity, but I was sure at least a few would question me, prod at my unyielding form, and try to figure out what was going on.

Then a good Samaritan would call the police. I'd likely be carted off to a human hospital, might be tested and analyzed by doctors who would find my blood work highly irregular...and highly intriguing at the same time.

At which point, the carefully nurtured secrecy protecting shifter society would really fall into disarray.

I didn't expect any amount of effort to speed up the unfreezing process. But, to my surprise, pins and needles of returning sensation prickled into my fingertips while I was still pondering the implications of my current dilemma. And by the time the last echo of retreating shifter steps rang out from the stairs behind my back, I was up and moving in the attacker's wake.

Immediately, my feet took two lunging steps forward, my lupine half itching to track down the bastard and give him a taste of his own medicine...then to figure out why in the world this city of ordinary shifters had attracted so many would-be rapists to its streets. But instead, I found myself sinking down onto my butt, never mind the nastiness that threatened to rub off the well-traveled concrete and onto my best pair of slacks. I didn't exactly descend into a sobbing heap of girlie goo. Still, I'll admit that a single tear streaked down the curve of my cheek and I allowed my attacker to make tracks with no attempt to chase him back down.

This isn't what my first adventure was supposed to turn into, I screamed silently inside my own head. The excitement of the journey shouldn't have descended into a jumble of ruined pastries, a missing brother who stood me up at every turn, and a pack of shifters who acted more like wolves than like men. I wasn't supposed to feel like such a *failure* seated amid a heap of fallen dreams.

Pulling out my phone, I stared at the smiling faces beaming back at me out of my digital address book. Despite the sinking sensation in the pit of my stomach, the array proved that I was never truly alone. Not when dozens of cousins and uncles and aunts would drop anything to come to my rescue...then never speak of the lapse again.

I couldn't contact any of them, though. Not when a mere breath of my predicament would send my father on a rampage, initiating an inter-pack battle that would tear our already splintered society apart. No, it was my turn to protect the pack...and that meant keeping my own counsel.

As if I'd called his presence into being, a new notification popped up on my display, halting my scroll through dozens of familiar faces. *Dad*, the caller ID read, and I smiled around the pain tightening my throat.

Predictably, Wolfie had sensed my moment of terror down the pack bond and had immediately picked up his phone to check in. It warmed my heart to possess a parent so perspicacious...but it also put me in a bit of a pickle.

Because I knew I couldn't leave Wolfie hanging. But I also didn't trust my equilibrium sufficiently to speak aloud when my father was bound to hear the tremble in my voice.

So when Wolfie followed up on his failed phone call with a short text—*"Are you alright?"*—I just tapped out a quick reply in the affirmative before powering the device down.

I wasn't dodging his calls. I was merely late to my meeting with the Greenbriar alpha. It was time to endear myself to the local pack.

CHIEF GREENBRIAR WAS surprisingly cordial when I showed up without either his son or a hostess gift...and fifteen minutes late to boot. The alpha's spouse, on the other hand, took an instant dislike to me that chilled the room by approximately twenty degrees in an instant.

"You have a little something right *here*," Andrea Greenbriar murmured, pointing to the spot above her left eyebrow. And even though she hadn't meant to draw my attention to her own blemish, I caught sight of a healing laceration that was still visible on the other woman's brow despite having been carefully caked over with concealer.

So Andrea was the female hunter whose toes I'd stepped on the night before. Not a good first impression...especially considering the fact that her mate intended to bring me into the family as their one and only daughter-in-law.

Of course, Aaron and I had formed an understanding to the contrary. Still, I immediately lifted my hand to pat at the offending area on my own head...and winced when my index finger came away streaked with frosting. Speaking of bad first impressions, turning up at a formal event dressed like a sugar-smeared baker definitely wasn't the introduction I'd meant to embrace.

My muscles tensed as the fight-or-flight reaction kicked in, and in response the faintest hint of a smirk curled Andrea's lips. She was mocking me...which was just the wrong approach to take if the female really *did* want to chase me out of her clan home.

Up until that point, my wolf had been resting inside our shared belly. But at the first sign of opposition, she woke, straightening my spine and moving my finger to pop one frosting-smeared digit into our human mouth. Rolling our tongue from side to side, we made a show of savoring the sugary concoction. "Mmm, delicious," I offered...then blanched as I realized I'd mimicked my own mugger's unfortunate terminology.

This time around, Chief Greenbriar was the one who picked up on my internal angst. "Is everything alright?" the older male asked, drawing me out of the crowd with one hand at the small of my back. And despite his ogling leer the first time we'd met in human form, the similarity of this alpha's words to those of my own father tempted me to open up. *I'm listening,* his stance told me. *Trust me,* added his inner wolf.

But I didn't fully understand the undercurrents currently flowing through this pack. So, instead of succumbing to the urge to over-share, I merely shook my head and offered: "Long day, no sign of my brother."

Then, since the pack leader and I had ended up in a secluded alcove where no one else would likely overhear our conversation, I took advantage of the moment to press my own case. "But I wanted to talk to you about something. Is now a good time...?"

"Of course," the alpha answered cordially, flagging down a passing waiter then pressing a tall flute of something alcoholic into my hand. "And I'll bet you'll feel better after a drink."

I *wouldn't* feel better post-imbibing, and I *would* need my wits about me when playing games with tricky werewolves. Still, I sipped obediently, the bubbles of a quality champagne tickling the inside of my nose. I barely managed to stifle a snort in reaction, proving that my sensitive palate was limited to baked goods alone.

Except my lack of sophistication was beside the point. Forgetting the champagne, I proceeded to launch into my own song and dance. "Something happened on my first night here, before I met you," I told the pack leader, going on to explain the bare bones of Harmony's near-rape combined with the scent of werewolf I'd found lingering around her apartment complex the very next day.

"Could you tell who the offender was?" Chief Greenbriar asked, his tone attentive yet calm. I wouldn't have dared tell a story like this to Wolfie without my mother in the room because Dad had been known to shift into lupine form the instant his protective instincts were aroused. Was my host's polished poise a sign that Chief Greenbriar possessed more control over his emotions than my hot-blooded father? I hoped so. Still, instinct told me to be vague, and I paid heed.

"It was dark and I was exhausted," I said by way of reply, telling the truth but not the whole truth and hoping my companion would spin the intended misunderstanding within his own head. "I know it's tough to do anything without being able to pin down who's at fault, but I was hoping you could still find a way to protect the human female? She has a pup and doesn't deserve to be harassed by dangers she can't possibly understand...."

"Of course. Consider it done." Chief Greenbriar's hand landed on my shoulder, the weight meant to be comforting but instead reminding me far too tangibly of my own near-rapist's touch. Only an effort of will locked me in place when both human and lupine halves of my character itched to wriggle free.

"Now tell me about my son," the pack leader continued. "And why he couldn't come out with you tonight."

This time, I didn't have to lie. "I have no idea what Aaron's up to," I answered, shrugging. "But he was polite when he dropped by to say he had to bail. I hope you won't hold it against him." *Or me,* I added silently.

Chief Greenbriar wanted to, I could tell. But even though he'd ordered my attendance at dinner tonight, he'd forgotten to require me to attend with his son in tow. And here I was, sipping champagne I clearly hated while appearing just as out of place as a baker tends to be at your average white-tie affair.

In the end, the city's alpha opted for fairness. "Tomorrow night, Aaron will be present," the older male promised.

Then a shifter hailed my companion from across the room and I was left alone in my corner of the busy party. Sticking the mostly full glass of champagne behind a planter, I slipped out the side door and hoofed it back to the empty subway station.

My duty was done. Now I could finally finish this seemingly endless day.

Chapter 15

Of course, Dad refused to be soothed by my half-hearted text. I should have guessed as much, but I was still surprised to find three missed calls from the male parental unit when I checked my phone on the walk up to Harmony's apartment building half an hour later. One I could have ignored, two might have been staved off with a second text...but three meant business.

Leaning my head against the smeared safety glass of the entranceway, I sighed and accepted that dealing with Wolfie's worry was a mandatory prerequisite for collapsing into my own bed. On the bright side, the scent of werewolf around the front door was fading, no additional shifters having passed by the spot since I walked out the door this morning. So that was one danger out of many that appeared to have become less tenacious than formerly anticipated.

Still, I wasn't quite ready to don a happy face for the sake of my discerning father. So, when my phone rang yet again, this time with my mother's name showing up on the screen, I decided to take the easy way out and use Mom as a conduit to Dad.

"Why are you avoiding your father?" Terra greeted me the instant I accepted her call. Rolling my eyes, I dropped down onto the concrete planter—devoid of life but full of cigarette butts—that marked one corner of the grungy doorway.

"I'm fine, Mom, and how are you?" I teased half-heartedly.

"Not so fine when I'm saddled with a worried mate," she muttered. I could almost see Mom's pursed lips and drumming fingernails. "Wolfie thinks you're mad at him. Want to tell me what's going on?"

"Mad at him?" And now I felt like the worst sort of scoundrel. I'd been evading my father's calls so Wolfie wouldn't show up on my doorstep with the cavalry in tow...and here Dad thought I'd somehow gotten pissed off enough to give him the silent treatment. How was it possible to hold a grudge against the teddy-bear/rottweiler hybrid that was my adopted dad? "I swear I'm not angry. Can you tell him that for me?"

"I'd make you tell Wolfie yourself, but your father's out putting the pups through their paces," Mom countered. Then, caving as she always did when faced with a potential breech in family cohesiveness, she added, "He'll be glad to hear you're doing well. Any sign of your brother?"

And that, likely, was what Dad really wanted to find out with his frequent calls anyway. Luckily, I trusted both of my parents with my life, so I downloaded every little detail...well, except for the nearness of my own miss earlier in the evening. Okay, and I might have left out my supposed engagement and the crazy attraction I felt for a human professor too. But other than that, I told her everything.

Mostly.

Mom was no dummy—she knew I was sidestepping key points. But unlike Dad, Terra wasn't adept at pushing the right buttons to get me to spill. So, after a few minutes of increasingly idle chitchat, she finally let me go.

And even though I hadn't told the whole truth and couldn't feel the Haven pack through the invisible tether that bound us together, I climbed the stairs with renewed energy. Because just touching base with home had put a spring back into my step. Meanwhile, as I exited the stairwell at the proper level, I could hear Rosie's laughter creeping out from underneath the Garcia door.

The portal in question opened before I even had time to knock, and my favorite toddler ran out crowing "She's here!" in baby-ese. Okay, so I'm totally guessing at the words. But the sentiment was obvious. Regardless of the details, the sight of welcoming faces was sufficient to carry tired feet over the last few paces between the outside world and my current safe harbor.

Today I'd baked and fought and hunted and lied. And now, at last, I was home.

"WE DON'T HAVE PIZZA for dinner every night," Harmony informed me, biting her lip as if she expected to be judged for lackadaisical culinary decisions. "But the lawyer I work for just won a big case, which means I get tomorrow off with pay. This is a celebration."

Rosie babbled something that sounded like "sick bay" but might have actually been a repeat of her mother's final word. Grinning, I pulled the sticky mass of pudgy limbs and boundless energy into my lap and snuggled her close while eying the final slice of pizza in the box. Maybe I should consume that lonely triangle of cheese and dough...just to make my hostess feel better about not cooking from scratch, of course.

There were only three of us sitting on the floor around the coffee table at the moment, the matriarch having disappeared into her room the moment I walked through the door. And despite the momentary wet blanket the older woman's absence caused, our celebratory mood was now so powerful that I had a hard time reminding myself that these people weren't pack.

Well, back home I would have honored a success by baking. So even though my legs ached and my eyelids drooped, I leveraged Rosie down onto her bare feet and padded into the tiny kitchen in search of supplies.

"What are you looking for?" Harmony asked, coming up to stand behind my left shoulder. She and I were still getting to know each other, so my companion left three more inches of air separating us than rightfully belonged. Still, the human's voice was easy when she added: "If you're still hungry, I think there's leftover stew in the fridge."

I opened the door of the appliance in question, but I wasn't looking for stew. Instead, I pulled out a jug of milk and a carton of eggs, then went hunting other baking paraphernalia in the nearby cupboards.

"Which do you like better—cookies or cake?" I asked Rosie after ascertaining that the bare minimum ingredients for each were indeed present. Then, realizing my mistake, I swung around to face her mother instead. "Except I'm betting it's past Rosie's bedtime and maybe she's not allowed to have sweets anyway...." The human metabolism, I knew, made werewolf-level consumption of sugar unrealistic.

But Rosie was already dancing around my feet shouting "kak, kak, kak!" at the top of her lungs. Oh boy—I'd created a monster. I winced as I raised pleading eyes to the mother who was bound to shoot us both down.

Only, she didn't. Instead, Harmony flicked on some music and lifted Rosie up to twirl around in the small space. Then, setting the munchkin down on the counter beside my baking gear, my hostess put me out of my misery.

"Usually this *would* be too late for dessert. But I don't have to work tomorrow, so I can stay up and wait out Rosie's sugar high. Plus," my companion said, lowering her voice and leaning in closer, "we never get homemade treats. Mama doesn't approve and I'm a terrible baker."

"You won't be after tonight," I promised, donning my teaching hat and feeling excitement course back into my veins at the same time. Harmony needed to know how to whip up something delicious at the drop of a hat—that was an essential life skill. "This recipe is so easy I could make it in my sleep. Actually, I think I did make it in my sleep once," I clowned, causing my smallest helper to hoot with laughter.

Of course, happy toddlers are clumsy toddlers. In her merriment, Rosie kicked her heels with delight....and knocked the entire carton of eggs off the counter. Only quick shifter reflexes managed to nab the container before its contents splattered all over the kitchen tiles.

That was a close one—in more ways than one. Glancing at Harmony out of the corner of one eye, I was glad to see the human's attention had been sidetracked by holding her daughter steady on her elevated perch, causing Harmony to miss out on my supernatural speed.

Time for a bit of distraction.

"Here, how about you take pictures?" I offered, pulling out my cell phone and swapping it for the container of salt Rosie was about to upend. Sure enough, the human toddler was just like the pups back home—obsessed with the idea of taking selfies—and the plaything became an immediate hit.

Child safely sedated, Harmony and I got to work...or rather, to play. Because despite baking for half the day already, moving around a tiny kitchen with my cheerful landlady filled my stomach with a strange sort of melty happiness not so different from the sensation I knew I'd get once the cake popped out of the oven and I imbibed the first steaming bite.

Of course, the kitchen was really too minuscule for two bakers. At first, we bumped into each other, laughing at our own clumsiness. But then something clicked and we were more dancing than cohabitating. Harmony's arm reached out to grab the measuring spoons and I instinctively leaned the other way to pluck flour out of the cupboard behind my back. We were on a roll.

"And that is how you bake a cake," I intoned in my most serious, professorial voice as we slid the second round pan into the hot oven. Harmony's cheeks were glowing and she appeared five years younger than when I'd first met her. Meanwhile, Rosie was still snapping photos with the vigor of a born paparazza.

"Let's see if you caught any good shots," my hostess said, pulling Rosie onto her hip and beginning to page back through the photos her daughter had recently taken. Predictably, the toddler reached forward to grab at the phone, and her mother tweaked the youngster's nose playfully while holding the device just out of reach.

But then fun fell away as Harmony's face paled. The other woman's chin rose and her brow furrowed, then she turned the screen around to face in my direction.

"Why do you have a picture of Derek on here?" my hostess demanded, her voice abruptly both brittle and cold. "Are you the reason he left his daughter behind?"

Chapter 16

No wonder Harmony and Rosie had felt like pack from the instant I met them. My hand trembled as I set down the butter knife I'd been using to test the doneness of the cake a moment earlier...a cake that suddenly appeared far less appealing than it had before my hostess dropped her verbal bomb.

"Kak, kak, kak!" Rosie chanted from her mother's arms. But the kid was bound to be disappointed, because no one was going to be eating cake anytime soon.

"Don't you move," Harmony told me, pointer finger extended and tone as adamant as that of any alpha werewolf. Then the human disappeared down the hallway, her voice softening as she soothed Rosie's fractious complaints before tucking the child into her crib to sleep.

For my part, the day's exhaustion fell back onto my shoulders like a ton of bricks, and I found myself sliding down the side of the counter to land on my butt on the newly mopped floor. I could smell cleaning agent all around me, the chemicals far too strongly scented to ever be used in a shifter household. And I imagined for a second that my brother had sat in this exact same spot, trying to decide what to do with a human woman he'd impregnated in complete disregard for the rules of shifter-kind.

A shiver ran down my spine as I—like he—considered the consequences. Chief Greenbriar didn't seem like the type to fold humans into his pack against the mandates of nation-level werewolf law. Instead, the alpha would have ordered Derek executed for his crimes, slaying Rosie and Harmony right along with him. No wonder my brother had stopped returning my chat requests....

Shaking my head to clear it, I reminded myself that the alpha would have killed Harmony and her daughter *first* since loose human lips presented a much greater danger than Derek's reckless dick. And *that* was an even worse thought than the initial one. The image of Rosie's lifeless body splayed out across the white floor filled my mind, the vision of toddler blood running down the cracks between the tiles so vivid that I reached out as if to touch the stain.

Abruptly, the cupcakes and cookies and pizza I'd eaten earlier that day didn't sit right in my stomach and I barely made it to the toilet before everything came back up in a stream of foul-tasting regret. Rosie was a bit over a year old, which meant it had been roughly twenty-four months since my niece was conceived. Coincidence that Derek had tracked me down at nearly the exact same time...or the beginning of a plan I had yet to fully understand?

"Please tell me you're not knocked up," Harmony demanded from behind my back, her words startling me into stillness. I couldn't believe she'd managed to creep up on me unnoticed while I was vomiting into the toilet bowl, but I guess I had enough on my mind to explain the slip.

To my surprise, my hostess's hands were kind as she pulled hair away from my face and wiped my neck with a damp washcloth. Then, in a further display of unwarranted generosity, she handed over a cup of water to clear the acid out of my mouth.

Despite her lack of overt anger, I still opted not to stand in Harmony's presence. Instead, I kept my eyes carefully averted as I accepted the liquid, and I took my time as I went through the motions of swish and spit.

Finally, though, I was forced to speak. "Not knocked up," I promised. Then, taking a deep breath, I told my companion the parts of the truth that were mine to give away. "Derek is my brother. Which, I guess, makes Rosie my niece."

For a moment, my throat tightened again, but this time from an emotion I'd never before felt. I adored my pack, cherished every single one of the people both in and out of Haven who had wriggled their way into my heart and turned themselves into my family moments after I was born. And yet...none of those clan members shared my blood.

Well, that wasn't technically true—Wolfie did. In a convoluted display of family fucked-up-ness that rivaled seventeenth-century royal families, our pack leader was technically my uncle in addition to being my chosen father. Because my birth dad had been Wolfie's brother...until our pack ran the former through with a sword, that is.

Other than Wolfie, though, I'd never before touched a living soul whose chromosomes shared so many alleles with my own. Was our genetic similarity the reason why Rosie's sweet little fingers had felt like a benediction every time they poked me in the eye?

I only remembered that Harmony was still present when the human dropped down into a squat by my side. "So where is he?" she demanded, her voice no longer furious, but anger still simmering beneath the words.

And it was at that moment that I realized Harmony was family too. She was my sister-in-law, I decided, marriage or no. Then, as I shortened the term to "sister" in my mind, warmth refilled the belly I'd so recently emptied of both dinner and lunch.

Still, when I gazed into my hostess's face at last, I winced. No, Harmony wasn't going to be pulling me to her bosom and welcoming me into her family anytime soon.

"I don't know," I answered at last, wishing I had something more salubrious to report. "That's why I'm here—trying to track him down. I actually had no clue Derek found a m...." I paused. "A wife and daughter. Running into you was just a fluke."

"Not such a fluke," Harmony answered, inhaling deeply through her nose before explaining. "Derek was a bus guy. Whenever he traveled, he always came home on the Greyhound. So I changed my routes to go past the station whenever I could, just in case." She paused, then added: "And we're not married."

Her emphasis on the final point suggested she thought it actually mattered, as if a human legal ceremony was responsible for anything beyond lowering a mated pair's tax bill. But, looking into Harmony's eyes, I saw more than a two-legger's need for formality. Instead, confusion and hurt glowed forth, along with stark uncertainty about her relationship with Derek that cut me to my very core.

I wanted to tell my sister that she was wrong, that Derek adored his mate and pup. But...my brother had never so much as mentioned their existence during our long hours of video chat. He hadn't moved into this apartment, which smelled nothing like moss, not even in the dusty corners where no one had thought to scrub. And he hadn't left any contingency plans in place to support a woman who should mean more to him than his own skin.

So maybe Harmony was right about Derek. But that didn't mean she lacked a clan. "You're my sister," I told her, reaching out one hand to pat her knee. The contact calmed my human side and soothed my wolf all at once. But then my eyes widened as I realized the disaster I'd unwittingly set into motion just a few hours earlier.

Because assuming he was true to his word, Chief Green-briar would come sniffing around this apartment soon, seeking the stalker who had threatened my sister the previous night. Would the alpha smell what I had missed—that my brother's sperm was responsible for the baby napping in the other room? Would "Top Dog" pull the Garcias into his pack...or would he take the easy way out and slay the humans to maintain the sanctity of shifter-kind?

I digested the danger for a split second, then I made my decision. "You're my sister," I repeated. "And you have to move. Tonight."

PREDICTABLY, HARMONY refused to obey my ultimatum. Equally predictably, she thought I was nuts to even suggest such a thing.

"We can talk more about this tomorrow," the human interjected when my words disintegrated into a pile of muddled explanation...that didn't, you know, actually *explain* anything. Then Harmony disappeared into the room already occupied by her mother and baby, leaving me no alternative save retreating back into my own space to gnaw on the issue alone.

And for the first few minutes, I tried to walk my worries away right there in my borrowed bedroom. But, let's be honest, pacing down a six-foot-long aisle partially obstructed by a chest of drawers on one side and an overhanging comforter on the other isn't entirely satisfying. Unsurprisingly, I soon found myself growing more frustrated rather than less so.

Meanwhile, my brain whirled through so many might-have-beens and may-bes that I wasn't really getting any rational thinking done. So, I turned around to twist the lock on the door behind my back, then I slipped out of my clothes and relaxed into the skin of my wolf.

In lupine form, the room brightened even as the intensity of colors dulled. Rosie's snuffling breathing and her grandmother's snores traveled easily from the other room, while the subtle rustle of Harmony tossing and turning suggested that my sister—like me—had ended the evening with more questions than answers running through her head.

At least she doesn't have to get up early tomorrow to go to work, I thought, salving my guilt for having dropped a bomb on my newfound sister without thinking up an adequate explanation to go along with it. Unfortunately, my own work schedule involved no such leeway. Not only was I expected at the coffee shop at eleven as usual, I had a full morning planned before my job even began.

Still, as a wolf, I understood that tomorrow would take care of itself. There was really nothing to be done except to finish out today.

To that end, I plopped down onto the bed, tucking my nose beneath my tail and forcing aching muscles to relax into somnolence. But my ears continued to twitch at every sound emanating from the other room, and the streetlight outside the window persisted in glaring directly into my sensitive eyes.

Rising, I turned in three tight circles to soften my nest, then flopped back down once again. But this time my own panting grated on my ears, fur itching all up and down my spine as my skin rebelled against mandatory solitude.

I needed pack. At home, I would have slipped outside my cottage door and howled once, then watched as cousins poured from their homes to join me on a midnight run. Or, if I'd really felt low, I could have crept inside my parents' home and jumped up into the tiny space between Terra's front and Wolfie's back. Sure, I was all grown up...but a wolf is never too old for a heart-felt cuddle.

I knew this would be a problem, I reminded myself. I'd hardened myself in preparation for the trip, resolving to run solo through the city no matter how welcoming the Greenbriar clan turned out to be. That was the way shifter society worked if I wanted to keep my nose clean and still make it home with no entanglements I'd later regret.

At the time, the task had appeared simple enough. And yesterday, I'd managed to fend off my urge for family despite the Greenbriar mantle tugging me to form a more permanent connection with the local pack.

Tonight, in contrast, my family was present in the very next room. A sister, a niece, and a grumpy old woman who I supposed must be my very first great-aunt.

Thumping my nose against the wall that lay between us, my wolf assessed how thin and breakable the barrier might be. Drywall—not so hard to tear through as long as we didn't run into a stud.

Whoa, there, I reined in my inner beast. Creepy stalker guests might open their hostess's door and peek inside in human form. In contrast, only monsters burst through the wall to lick at humans' sleeping faces.

But I *needed* pack so deeply that my claws tucked in and out like those of a cat. Slobber soaked the bedspread where I'd drooled out my distress and my ears pinned back against my skull. Finally giving in, I leapt to the floor and nosed at the pocket of flour-dusted work pants.

The phone glowed to life immediately, Derek's face shining up at me as it had done repeatedly throughout the day. This time, though, I winced and looked away, my brother's enigmatic smile suddenly more confusing than it was heartening.

Still, I managed to swipe over to the call function despite Derek's ambush, then I tapped at Dad's image on the screen. And, when Wolfie answered, voice scratchy with sleep, I whined out the thinnest trickle of sound by way of greeting.

"Buttercup," Wolfie murmured with no surprise or annoyance evident in his voice despite the late hour. He must have put some serious effort into our connection too, because as he spoke the Greenbriar mantle rippled and folded back out of the way. Then I could feel my father through our own pack bond, his incorporeal arms hugging me and filling my belly with wolf-imbued warmth.

"Go to sleep," my father crooned, his words descending into a lullaby. And, curled around the phone like a life line, I obeyed my alpha. Dropping chin onto paws, I went out like a light.

Chapter 17

Everything always looks brighter in the morning...especially after waking up in lupine form with the sound of my parents' steady breathing on the other end of the line. Shaking off my lupine skin and picking up the phone with human fingertips, I pressed the device to my ear with a genuine smile on my lips.

"Morning, Mom, Dad."

"Good morning, Buttercup," Wolfie answered, his voice a whisper. Muffled by distance, I could still make out the steady whistle of Terra's not-quite-snore in the distance, and I lowered my own voice to keep from waking my mother up.

"I know you want details, but I've got to hustle," I started, excuses more unwieldy when I had to spin them directly into my father's ear rather than through an intermediary.

But Wolfie didn't press the point. Instead, he offered the same unconditional support as always. "You know we're here if you need us," he rumbled...and as Dad spoke I realized there *was* something he could do to help me protect my newfound sister without putting everyone's noses out of joint.

"Actually...do you think you could track down a phone number? I know the Greenbriar pack almost certainly keeps theirs just as deeply unlisted as we do, but maybe...?"

Dad harrumphed as if he'd been insulted. "You ask that as if you're uncertain of my skills," he growled, reminding me that his day job was keeping businesses' computers safe from internet attack. "Give me a name and I'll have the number before you're done brushing your teeth."

Then he, rather than I, was the one to click off the phone. Grinning, I ran my tongue around the inside of my mouth, feeling the moss that had built up after failing to attend to basic dental hygiene the night before. Sometimes, I thought Dad was a mind reader—he certainly didn't miss a single trick.

So I texted over all the information I had available before creeping into the bathroom, carefully bypassing the cheerful voices that emanated from the other end of the hall in the process. And, sure enough, by the time I'd regained my usual minty fresh breath, Andrea Greenbriar's number sat on my phone's screen, just waiting to be used.

Only, now that the avenue had opened before me, the idea of using Andrea to fend off her mate seemed trickier than it had a few minutes earlier. Time to add a trace of self-assurance to my voice.

To that end, I pulled my most formal set of clothing out of my suitcase, slipping into a business suit that cupped my breasts and thighs while still making me feel more like a badass rather than a femme fatale. I even swiped on a coat of lipstick and splashed eyeshadow onto my lids. Then, sitting on the bed as primly as any society matron, I dialed the relevant number and waited for the alpha's mate to pick up.

The phone rang so many times I wasn't sure if the city's matriarch would even accept my call. But at last, Andrea answered, her voice both curt and cold. "Who is this?"

My number would have shown up on her phone as "unlisted," and it said something about the tenuousness of the female's current position that she'd bothered to answer at all. So I left her hanging for ten solid seconds to consolidate my perceived dominance. Then, one instant before Andrea would have ended our connection, I spoke. "We need to talk."

"We have nothing to talk about." Despite her terse response, though, Andrea didn't bother pretending ignorance. She recognized my voice, had likely expected a call like this for over a decade. How could she not when her family secret made the future appear so dark that she didn't dare peer further ahead than the following day?

It was hard not to feel sorry for a mother placed in such an impossible situation...especially when the future she feared was built upon old-fashioned beliefs as precarious as a house of cards. But Andrea had bought into the bunk and I needed leverage to protect my human sister and niece. So I played dirty. "With Aaron as your son...you really don't think we need to meet face to face?"

For one long moment, it appeared that I'd pressed too hard. Andrea's breathing grew harsh and loud on the other end of the line, and I could almost feel her wolf rising up behind human eyes. Sure enough, when she spoke at last, the words came out garbled around lupine fangs. "When and where?"

"The coffee shop on campus. 10:30," I answered. Then, feeling thoroughly dirty despite my recent shower, I ended the call.

I ALMOST LEFT THE ROOM as I was rather than digging out the gift Auntie Fen had given me at the beginning of my journey. After all, what good were physical weapons against a werewolf who could freeze me in place with a single word?

But, if nothing else, the knives would act as a physical connection to my absent family. So I unwrapped the slender blades with care then slipped each into a sheath, the first accessible through a slit in my pants pocket, the second around my ankle, and a third hidden alongside my spine. Assuming a shifter didn't get the jump on me so quickly I was unable to move my hands, I was ready for anything.

Well, I was ready for anything...save the two sets of accusing eyes that met mine when I stepped into the combined kitchen/dining room at last. Only my niece was still a member of the Ember fan club, as evidenced by the refrain of "Kak, kak, kak" she embarked upon while holding out a fistful of chocolate fluff in a sweet yet misguided attempt to share.

"No thanks, Rosie-Dozey," I told the child with forced cheer. But before I could pat my favorite munchkin on the head, her grandmother's cane rose one menacing inch off the floor and my hand snapped back against my side. *Uh oh.* "I've got to head to work," I explained to the downcast toddler as I changed my trajectory and backed quickly toward the door instead.

Unfortunately, the Garcia matriarch wasn't willing to let me escape so easily. "Tell her," the older woman demanded, the words aimed at her daughter even though her gaze continued to pierce me with arrow-like sharpness. And as a wordless exchange passed between the two adults, I could feel my future solidifying in the air.

An eviction from the premises, a complete inability to protect my family from danger, total divorce from the niece I'd known for only one short day. "Please," I started, not sure what I could possibly say to avert such profound disaster...from a werewolf's point of view at least.

Harmony opened her mouth to obey her mother's wishes. But before I could think of a single way to change my hostess's decision, the younger woman's teeth came together with a snap and she shook her head instead. "Ember and I can talk tonight," Harmony told us both after a moment of loaded silence. "I don't want to make her late for work."

The truth was, I had scads of time before I needed to open up shop, even possessed quite a bit of leeway before my appointment with Andrea Greenbriar. But I seized on the offered out like a drowning swimmer who'd been tossed a life line.

"Yes, right, I'm running late," I babbled, darting through the waiting doorway and into the hall. I didn't breathe easily until the heavy wooden barrier had slammed shut behind my back.

AT WHICH POINT I REALIZED that I lacked a key to the apartment I'd just left behind. If the Garcias failed to let me back in this evening, then I'd be stuck in the city without so much as a single change of clothes. Dad wouldn't be impressed by my dental hygiene then, now would he?

In which case I'll just buy new stuff, I decided. After all, panties and toothpaste were easily replaced. In contrast, the slender thread of possibility that I might still make things right with my sister-in-law trumped all else.

So, turning away from the door, I double timed it down the hallway and stairs before Harmony could change her mind and call me back for a much-deserved dressing down. Out in the morning air, I breathed in the dampness of a freshly washed city, overnight rain having swept away the scents of too many people and cars. I could smell grass and pollen and flowers for the first time since the Greenbriar hunt, the mild aromas mixing together to encircle me in a haze of welcome.

The subway was still dirty as ever, though, and my heart rate picked up as I passed through the empty station on the campus end after exiting my northbound train. This was where I'd been attacked yesterday, and the tang of my own terror still hung heavy on the subterranean air.

Rather than rushing out into the light and making the same mistake a second time, though, I slunk along pitted walls, scanning the open space between me and the exit. One hand slipped into my pants pocket, settling around the hilt of Auntie Fen's knife, and in response my breathing gradually eased to normal levels once again.

Only when I felt able to survey my surroundings with the mind of a predator rather than prey did I advance out into the open. My attacker wasn't present, of course. No matter what they say about perpetrators returning to the scene of the crime, only an idiotic werewolf would linger in the spot where he'd nearly raped a pack princess. Especially when his victim possessed guest rights granted by the local alpha himself.

In contrast to the dangerous scene I'd been envisioning, in fact, the campus was bright and cheerful beneath the morning sun. I passed two of the previous day's customers as I skirted the main administrative building, and another waved hello as I used my key to enter the coffee shop. There, I flipped the lock closed behind me and finally relaxed into a round of baking therapy.

First, I pulled together apple turnovers for Andrea—might as well sweeten the female up as reparation for my upcoming blackmail. Then, with a smile, I beat together a batch of the super-fluffy cupcakes that were Dad's favorite. After all, Wolfie deserved a culinary thank-you in exchange for his endless offerings of surprisingly hands-off support.

While the cupcakes cooled, I created a mailing box out of taped-together take-out trays then penned a quick note for my mother and pack. Without bothering to lock the door behind me, I trotted back across campus the way I'd come and turned into the mail room that sat only a few hundred yards away from the subway station. There, a wall of small metal boxes ended in a counter manned by one very bored human clerk.

"What can I get you?" the employee asked, his eyes remaining trained on the magazine in his lap. Then, looking up at last, the clerk's eyes brightened as he recognized me from his visit to my shop the day before. "You're the cupcake girl! Want to open up a PO box? Faculty, students, and staff all get one free of charge."

"That's nice of you," I answered, glancing at the clock above the clerk's head and realizing I was cutting it closer than I'd intended with regard to Andrea's appointment. "But I'm not sure how long I'll be in town. I just need to mail this one thing...."

Luckily, the human required only thirty seconds to calculate postage and accept my payment, then I was trotting back the way I'd come. Past the library, through a little grove of evergreens, then around the bend that hid my shop from view...

...At which point I walked directly into the arms of last night's attacker.

Chapter 18

He hesitated before going on the offensive, and that was the only mistake I needed in order to launch my counterattack. Whirling, I yanked a knife out through the slit in my pocket and slashed at the meaty hands reaching for my throat. Red blood arced away from my opponent's flesh, ruby droplets glinting on the steel of my blade before turning dark as they splattered across the perfectly manicured grass.

The other shifter swore but didn't retreat. Instead, he groped around at the small of his own back and drew forth something far more dangerous than my own throwing knives—the cold, hard weight of a gun.

Auntie Fen was right after all, I thought with a shiver. Because my aunt had *tried* to hand over a highly-illegal pistol rather than the three mostly-legal knives I'd ultimately accepted. She'd told me that toeing the line of human laws might not work out in my favor outside Haven's walls, that guns hadn't been illegal long enough to have dropped off the average criminal's radar.

"But what if a human cop stops me and demands a body search? What then?" I'd asked her.

"So don't do something stupid enough to get on their radar," Auntie Fen had countered.

Now I regretted brushing off advice from someone older and wiser than myself. I'd been leery of carrying a handgun when possession alone was sufficient to send non-military personnel straight to jail. But getting shot by a shifter suddenly seemed like a much worse alternative...and significantly more likely too.

The shock of staring down the barrel of a pistol, in fact, sent words tumbling out of my mouth before I could weigh them against the requirements of good sense. "What do you think you're doing?" I demanded. "Are you *trying* to get the human police involved?"

Unsurprisingly, my opponent didn't answer. Instead, he widened his stance, bringing his second arm around to steady the first as he sighted along the top of the gun. The easy familiarity with which he held the pose suggested that this wasn't any stolen weapon. Instead, my opponent had likely practiced with and experimented upon this pistol until he wielded it like an extension of his own skin. *Bad news.*

"Drop the knife and go inside," my opponent told me after one long moment, backing up his command with a jerky gesture of his shallow chin. But he didn't speed me along my way with an alpha compulsion like the one he'd slapped onto me the night before. Was the oversight merely due to confidence that I'd already been beaten, I wondered, or was there another reason behind eschewing his own werewolf strength this morning?

Either way, I wasn't about to walk into what was bound to be an ambush. So, taking care to slump my shoulders and keep my eyes averted in a show of submission, I nonetheless refused to budge. "I can't drop a blood-stained knife on the grass on a human campus. Think for a minute about where we are and who's around. Chief Greenbriar will gut us both if we're responsible for cluing in one-bodies to our presence."

Rather than reasoning with me, my opponent growled and took a single step closer, prompting hairs to rise along the back of my neck. My mind raced as I assessed options, finding each one less palatable than the last. Because every potential solution I dreamed up ended in the exact same way—with shifter blood analyzed in a human hospital where doctors were bound to notice the oddities of werewolf metabolism and DNA. The potential for discovery was more daunting than the current risk to my own skin.

"Don't..." I started. Then a cool, feminine hand landed on my left shoulder blade and cut into my desperate plea.

"*Enough*," Andrea Greenbriar intoned, her word encompassing us both and pushing all air out of my lungs in the process. Rather than looking in my direction, though, she chided the male werewolf for his overstep. "I merely asked you to ensure Ember wasn't armed," she said, her words quiet but their intensity nonetheless prompting her underling to look away submissively while tucking the gun back underneath his clothes.

Then the female's piercing gaze turned on me, cold air spiraling around my face as her displeasure made itself known. "And *you*," Andrea murmured, "*you* should know better than to come to a meeting with knife in hand."

It was patently unfair to accuse me of being armed when her own bodyguard boasted the more dangerous weapon and had been the first to attack. Still, I kept my mouth shut and instead tried to figure out how much of today's kerfuffle was co-incidental...and how much pointed at another, deeper game.

Had Andrea's bodyguard really acted against her wishes, both today and last night? Was there a reason the male had been able to use an alpha compulsion on me then but not now?

Puzzles pieces clicked together in my mind, but gaping holes continued to mar my understanding of the situation. However, since the female before me was obviously powerful enough to force me to jump off the top of a building if she so desired, I figured there was only one truly important issue to deal with at the present moment.

My companion needed that apple turnover sooner rather than later.

So, flipping my knife around until I gripped the bloody blade instead of the handle, I extended the hilt in her general direction. "My apologies, alpha. I only came to talk."

Andrea had been willing to tear out the throat of an elk with her own lupine fangs two nights earlier, but her lip curled in disdain now as she took in the red smears and greasy sweat that streaked the recently handled hilt. "Keep it," she told me. Then, speaking to her underling as if to a dog, she intoned an unnecessary compulsion: "*Stay.*" Finally, turning on her heel, Andrea Greenbriar strode back into my shop, allowing the glass door to settle closed behind her with a whoosh of displaced air.

For a moment, the bodyguard and I eyed each other with stark distrust coloring both of our faces. Then, with a shrug, I wiped the sullied blade on the inside of my shirt where the stain wouldn't show before slipping the weapon back into its holster.

It took an effort of will to turn my back on an armed were-wolf who had attempted to maul me only eighteen hours earlier and had considered shooting me today. But I clenched my jaw and raised my chin. Then, ignoring my own trepidation, I followed the alpha's mate into my own chocolate-scented shop.

"I'LL TAKE A LARGE COFFEE, cream and no sugar," Andrea informed me the moment I entered the space. She was seated at a corner booth where she could watch all activity both outside and inside while being largely hidden in shadows herself. Despite the less-than-adequate lighting, though, my lupine eyes could pick my opponent out quite admirably.

And as I filled the female's order, my surreptitious glances proved that she wasn't nearly as poised as she wanted to appear. Instead, one shoe tapped repeatedly against the floor tiles even as her fingernails drummed against the table top three feet above. Meanwhile, Andrea's gaze slid in my direction far too frequently to maintain her pretense of aloof boredom.

No, the conclusion was obvious—despite her heavy-handed tactics, my current companion was a devoted mama worried about her adult pup. I couldn't let her off the hook entirely, but I still slid a pastry onto a plate and carried it over along with the requested coffee. "I hope you like apple turnovers," I murmured as I took my own seat on the other side of the scuffed tabletop.

For a split second, my companion's face softened as the scent of cinnamon rose between us. But rather than digging in, Andrea ignored the treat and got right down to business.

"If you threaten my son, you threaten me," she intoned, eyes boring into mine so dangerously they sent my inner wolf whimpering for cover. And between the lines, I read the rest of the threat as easily as if it had been voiced aloud. *Being mugged in a public setting isn't the worst that can happen*, Andrea's eyes informed me. *Last night and this morning were warnings. Don't force my hand.*

Growling very faintly under my breath, I accepted her words for the admission of guilt they were. And I was very tempted to reply in kind, maybe offering up a verbal slap that reminded Andrea of my own pack's power.

But that would have been counterproductive...especially since I was currently acting under my own volition and without any nearby relatives to back me up. So I merely shrugged and pointed at her turnover. "If you don't want that, I can get you something else."

Closing her eyes in momentary frustration, human politeness eventually won out over Andrea's lupine urge to dominate. The alpha werewolf raised the pastry to her lips with the daintiness of a debutante...and, ever so gradually, the power of spicy apples began relaxing her tensed muscles.

Here's the thing about apple turnovers. They don't look like much compared to a triple-chocolate-chunk cupcake with a drizzle of syrup across the top. And yet, the treat's melding of apple, sugar, and cinnamon proves that a chef doesn't need dozens of complicated ingredients to create something truly divine.

At her core, Andrea was similarly simple. She was a hunter, a mother, and a mate. And while I'd brought the female here as a mother, it was the hunter I wanted to tap into now.

So I waited until the sugared fruit had sweetened my companion's temperament, then I let her parental instincts off the hook. "I'm not going to say anything about Aaron," I informed her. "That's his own personal business...although, if I was sticking my nose in, I think he and Roger make a pretty good match."

For a moment, Andrea's eyes flashed with anger. I'd brought the city's second most powerful werewolf here under false pretenses and we both knew it. Still, it was hard for a mother to fight against open-armed acceptance of her pup, so after a moment her inner wolf stood down.

"Then what *do* you want?" Andrea asked carefully, sipping at her coffee and forgetting to scan for danger this time as she nibbled another bite out of her rapidly disappearing turnover. Not that there was likely to be anything worth guarding against on this college campus...well, except for the barely leashed bodyguard she herself had brought along.

"I want protection for a family of humans," I answered once Andrea's eyes returned to my face, only to be interrupted before I could get another word out.

"The Garcias?" my companion asked, eyebrows rising. "Arnold told me you were concerned about them. He'll send a few men to look over the situation this afternoon. But I have to say, it's already under control." *And not worth blackmailing me about*, my companion's accusing eyes added.

"Well, here's the thing," I answered. "I don't want him to send out any *men*. As you well know, the males in this city are having trouble keeping their paws to themselves."

Because I didn't entirely buy Andrea's implication that her bodyguard had attacked me the previous evening under her own overt orders. Sure, the female had learned about her underling's lapse and had used that knowledge to intimidate me today...but I suspected she'd neither commanded nor approved of his actions at the time.

I'd yet to figure out exactly *why* the bodyguard attacked me yesterday, and I had similar questions about Roger's actions the night before. But I was close to tracking down answers. And in the meantime, I couldn't afford any loose cannons sniffing around Harmony's apartment, nor did I want Chief Greenbriar sussing out Rosie's connection to my missing sibling if the toddler happened to step outside and into the jaws of a supposedly protective wolf.

So I ignored Andrea's glare and barreled right into the solution I'd come up with the night before. "I won't tell anyone about Aaron and I'll continue pretending like he's mate material. But you have a problem within your own clan. After setting a *female* guard on my landlady, I recommend you track down the source of your pack's rotten core."

Chapter 19

Despite the drama of the morning, the rest of my work day proved surprisingly uneventful. The brownie-eating professor brought in his wife...who was plump and cheerful and didn't complain one bit about her husband's dietary preferences. Meanwhile, yesterday's female students returned with three friends in tow, and the shop gradually began to feel more like a cheerful meeting place and less like the cold, silent corner of campus it had initially appeared.

Feeding the masses warmed the cockles of my heart...but I still grew increasingly jittery as the day progressed. It was hard to remain in one place while my mind ran in several different directions at once, none of which involved pastries and all of which reeked of potential danger. So, at 3 pm, I dialed the same number I'd called far too often throughout the day, hoping for yet another status report on my absent sister.

"Still no trouble," Lissa answered, not bothering to wait for my question this time around. The female shifter and her partner had been stationed outside Harmony's apartment building within fifteen minutes of Andrea leaving my own premises, and their calm assurance should have dismissed all worries about my sister-in-law's safety. And yet...I still harbored a sinking suspicion that something was going wrong out in the city while I whipped up frosting and poured cream into coffee cups within my insulated bubble here on campus.

"Are you positive?" I asked for the sixth time that day. Then racking my brain in an effort to guess what the stationed guards might have missed, I added: "What about the side entrance?"

"Marcia is standing right in front of it. And before you ask, neither of us has seen or smelled a hint of fur since we got here. This isn't the shifter side of town. You can relax."

Lissa's frustration was evident in her clipped sentences, and I couldn't really blame her. Staking out a human apartment building was a pretty low-level chore, and it wasn't fair of me to suggest the shifters in question weren't up to the job. Still....

"What about the roof? Would you be able to see if anyone took an aerial approach?"

"Have you even been here?" Lissa snapped back, her politeness finally wearing thin. "There's no way to access the roof short of a helicopter. And I can *promise* you, I would hear a chopper if hypothetical miscreants tried to fly in and nab a *human* out from under my nose."

"Okay," I answered, dropping my head into one hand and letting the issue drop. The other shifter was right—I was being overprotective and a total pain in the butt.

So, after a much-needed apology, I forced myself to hang up the phone. I didn't call to check in for the next two hours. And when quitting time rolled around, I didn't take advantage of my spare hour between work and mandatory Greenbriar dinner to rush home and check on Harmony's defenses as I'd initially intended.

Instead, I accepted the fact that the Garcia family was being guarded by pack. Since I'd also run out of avenues to explore with regard to Derek's disappearance, I chose not to spin my wheels and instead headed in the one direction bound to soothe my tattered temperament.

I'd take Sebastien up on his invitation and drop by his office. The decision had nothing to do with the molten chocolate coloration of the human's eyes, nor with his absence from the shop today. Instead, I told myself I was merely looking forward to talking about something other than werewolves for a change.

LIKE THE REST OF CAMPUS, the college's psychology building was nearly empty at quitting time on a summer evening. So I wandered down dimly lit corridors for several minutes, searching for the room number from Sebastien's card. And as I skimmed research posters lining the endless hallways, my eye snagged upon the long list of funders who had supported even the simplest of experiments.

Dad would have laughed at all the ten-dollar names, and I couldn't resist perusing them now as I ambled past. I was vaguely familiar with the National Institute of Science and the Defense Advanced Research Projects Agency (or DARPA for short), but even the private scholarship funds seemed to require listings up to a dozen words long.

"Dorothy E. and Kenneth C. Upton Foundation," I read aloud, trying to decide whether the couple had been clowning around by creating an acronym that turned into an invective when read backwards...or whether they'd just missed out on the joke. Humor aside, Derek—with his lone wolf's obsession for making ends meet—might have been attracted to the seemingly endless funds made available by well-heeled college alums. Was my brother's obsession with the campus merely an attempt to support his lavish lifestyle without having to sign on with an established pack?

The idea made intuitive sense...yet it still didn't quite ring true. Maybe I just didn't want to turn my brother into either a desperate loner or a money-grubbing scam artist, but my gut told me there was more to Derek's interest in the college than the mere need for easy financing.

The answer, I suspected, lay with the key tucked away in my pocket. Fingering the cool metal, I considered trying it in every knob I passed. Surely the answer to Derek's disappearance lay here on the campus he'd talked so much about.

And yet...how many doors existed in this building alone? And how many other parts of the city had Derek mentioned in passing during our dozens of chats? No, I needed to come up with a more structured approach to the current investigation or I'd continue getting nowhere fast.

Meanwhile, I turned a corner and discovered that the room numbers lining the hallway were finally heading in the proper direction. The clack of fingers on a keyboard drew me yet deeper into the complex, then I forgot all about my brother as I peeked through an open doorway and caught sight of the back of Sebastien's enticing head.

I knew the professor could never be anything more to me than an intriguing acquaintance, but my breath still caught as I took in the sunlight glinting through my companion's short yet tangled locks. My muscles relaxed for the first time all day as his scent wafted into my nostrils. And for an instant, my lupine half closed its eyes and sighed in contentment, as if we'd returned from a lone hunt to snuggle into the heart of our chosen pack.

Focus, Ember, I reminded myself. I wasn't here to be sucked in by masculine beauty and I definitely wasn't here to find a mate. I was hunting for my brother, and to that end I forced myself to tear my eyes away from Sebastien's muscular form and peruse his workspace instead.

Unfortunately, what I saw made the human more intriguing rather than less so. Because the room was awash with plants. A well-trained ficus arched around the side of one large window while spider plants spawned babies in hanging baskets above his head. Along the opposite wall, a fish tank burbled with life, colorful swimmers darting out from amid the fronds of pond plants while colorful snails slimed their way up the insides of the glass surfaces.

"It looks like you'd rather be outside," I said aloud, forgetting for a moment that my companion wasn't a shifter and thus wouldn't have heard me approach. Sure enough, Sebastien's entire body jolted at the sound of my voice, his head swiveling toward me like that of a startled deer assessing its surroundings. But then a broad smile lit the professor's face as he caught sight of me hovering in the entranceway.

"Ember," he greeted me. "Come on in."

Chapter 20

I'd meant to use the seconds before being noticed to build some sort of internal wall against Sebastien's overwhelming charm. But, instead, the warmth in my companion's voice was as effective as any alpha compulsion. Muscles moved without conscious volition, and before I knew it I'd skittered through the doorway and right up into his personal space.

Only then did my companion realize that I had no place to sit. Which meant I missed out on the handshake I'd been looking forward to all day, although I *was* graced with an excellent view of Sebastien's well-formed backside as he turned to scoop a stack of well-thumbed periodicals out of the visitor's chair.

"I'm afraid I've spread my research out over every available surface," the professor mumbled as he worked. "I don't get many drop-bys in the summertime..."

Then his voice trailed off as his cheeks turned ever so faintly red. In response, I nearly laughed aloud, realizing the human I'd thought unflappable was embarrassed to be caught with his office in disarray.

"Please don't clean on my account," I told him. Reaching out without thinking, I placed two fingertips on Sebastien's wrist in a werewolf gesture of consolation....then lost track of what I'd meant to say as the momentary contact pushed all further conversation out of my mind.

Because Sebastien's blood pulsed beneath the pads of my fingers, his heart beating just a little faster than it ought to have done. His skin was warm, his scent mild compared to that of a werewolf but strangely enticing nonetheless. And when I gazed into the professor's eyes, I noticed his pupils were dilating...just like my own despite the more-than-adequate light.

By the time my hand slipped away from my companion's skin, I was barely verbal. So I dropped down into the newly emptied chair rather than opening my mouth. No need to let potentially embarrassing words spew forth while my equilibrium was so thoroughly compromised.

"Did you come for the..." Sebastien began, then cleared his throat before continuing. "...for the candy bar?"

"I...yes, of course."

I hadn't, actually. I'd forgotten all about my companion's request that I take part in his study, hadn't given so much as a passing thought to the promised sugar rush and cash prize in exchange for relinquishing half an hour of my time. Instead, I'd been drawn to this plant-filled study by an instinct too powerful to resist...and definitely far too complicated to explain to a human I'd barely met.

Still, I'd cling to any excuse that allowed me to spend extra time in Sebastien's presence. So I didn't argue when my companion launched into what sounded like a well-rehearsed spiel, and I nodded sagely when he told me the study had to be carried out in pairs.

"Just give me a sec to text the participant at the top of the waiting list," the professor said absently, matching actions to words. Then, piercing me yet again with those un-look-away-able eyes, he stilled my lungs with another breathtaking smile.

"We're in luck. Gracie says she can be here in just a few minutes."

After that, the professor leaned back in his chair while I perched awkwardly on the edge of my own seat. A mere four feet of empty space separated us, but the distance felt more like a yawning abyss rather than the width of a rather book-and-plant-crowded study.

For thirty excruciatingly long seconds, in fact, we each made an earnest effort to be polite and not to stare. Then we both opened our mouths to speak at once.

"Did you ever...?" he asked just as I started with "Why did you...?"

We both paused, mouths snapping shut in tandem. Then Sebastien's warm brown eyes crinkled with mirth as he placed a finger over his own lips, dropped his chin into his chest, and waited for me to finish my thought.

"Why did you choose to go into psychology?" I said into the resulting silence. Then I immediately wanted to kick myself as I realized the question was far too nosy for two humans who had only recently met.

But rather than taking offense, my companion merely shrugged. "For the same reason you bake, I imagine," he answered. And I found myself scooting backwards in my seat, surprised to have been so thoroughly *seen* by a human who hadn't visited my shop more than a single time.

Because Sebastien was right. I baked to understand. I baked to assist. I baked to be needed.

I opened my mouth to question a human who sounded more like a werewolf than many shifters I knew. But a tap on the door burst the bubble of privacy that surrounded us, and

I looked up to find one of my own customers leaning into the doorway from the otherwise empty hall.

"GRACIE, THANKS FOR joining us," Sebastien greeted her, rising so quickly that I was left wondering whether our moment of shared understanding had existed entirely within my own head. The professor was all business as he ushered us back out into the hall, but his physical and emotional distance didn't prevent the student from thrusting out her chest and simpering prettily as she followed his lead.

She's a pup and he's an alpha, I reminded myself, trying to tamp down the wave of lupine jealousy that threatened to overwhelm my human body. I couldn't blame the girl for trying to attract our companion's attention, never mind that both age and profession placed Sebastien firmly out of her league. Still, I found myself sidling around so that I, rather than Gracie, was standing at Sebastien's elbow when he stopped at last inside the sparsely furnished lab.

And who's the lovesick pup now?

Luckily, the professor appeared as oblivious to our competitive maneuvering as he had been to the wares Gracie put so flagrantly on display. Instead of remarking on either, he launched into a long-winded explanation of the apparatus before us, which had apparently been designed with dozens of safeguards in mind.

"As I told Gracie when she first signed up," the professor concluded, strapping electrodes onto various portions of the girl's anatomy as he spoke, "our lab is studying pain tolerances this summer. The participant who sits in this chair—that would be Gracie—will be subjected to increasing voltages of electrical shock...."

And, abruptly, the fizz of attraction winked out as I realized what sort of study this really was. Sebastien's breezy manner when introducing the chair had suggested we were in for something simple and harmless, maybe virtual-reality puzzles or a team-building exercise. Instead, my brain went entirely blank as I tried to come up with a different explanation for what I'd recently heard.

Was this man—who I'd pegged as gentle and kind—really planning to *harm* a pup barely old enough to leave her parents? To send electrical currents pulsing through Gracie's veins...for what purpose? To end up with a readout that would assist in the creation of yet more boring articles that only a few other scientists might ever read?

"I'm not sure..." I interjected, backing toward the door. But I *was* sure. I was sure I'd made a tremendous mistake, both in offering to take part in this study and in thinking the attraction I felt for Sebastien was worth the risk to both of our necks.

"Please don't go," the human countered, stepping so deeply into my personal space that his body heat brushed against my bare skin. And despite the horror that churned my stomach and tensed my muscles...I still found myself leaning closer to the professor rather than away.

"It's entirely safe," Sebastien continued. "I promise. And Gracie will be well compensated. She receives more than a candy bar for being the subject in the chair. You want to take part, don't you, Gracie?"

The professor's dark eyes bored into mine even as the student chirruped from behind his back. "Absolutely, professor. It's the highlight of my day."

She really did seem to mean it too, so I exhaled a long breath and turned away from Sebastien with an effort. "You *want* to do this?" I asked the younger female, brow wrinkling as I tried to understand the nonsensical undercurrents filling the lab. There was more going on here than a puppy-dog crush, but I couldn't quite put my finger on what I was missing.

"Absolutely," the teenager answered. "'Cause you're here to make sure it's all safe and kosher. Tell her that part, professor."

And Sebastien immediately launched into the second half of his prepared explanation. I was the spotter, he explained, present to ensure Gracie's pain threshold was never exceeded. Before every pulse of electricity, the professor would ask his subject if she wanted to continue, but I was the one ultimately responsible for determining whether the electrifying button got pushed.

"So if I say no, you pull the plug?" I asked, making sure I understood. Part of me wanted to track down a member of the administration right away, to argue my case until this inhumane experiment was shut down both immediately and permanently. But Gracie peered up at me with such pleading in her youthful eyes, and Sebastien's further clarification suggested the study was no worse than my cousins' customary test of bravery—prodding at electrified fence wires back home until the current nipped at their skin. Surely this scientifically formulated shock wouldn't hurt more than the time I'd been conned into licking that fence with my unprotected tongue....

"It would be a big favor to me if you'd help out," Gracie interjected, looking even more childlike as she pouted plump lips and stared at me with widened eyes.

And, at last, I caved. Utilizing my werewolf senses, I'd be able to assess the girl's pain threshold far more effectively than a one-body could have done. Perhaps taking part in this experiment wasn't the same as assisting in torture.

Perhaps.

The experiment moved quickly after that. Sebastien stood in front of Gracie, his finger hovering atop a big red button, while I was placed in a chair off to one side. And the girl really didn't seem to mind the initial shocks—which Sebastien explained were less painful than even a pinprick, intended to calibrate the sensors and ensure everything was advancing according to plan.

But then the professor turned up the dial on his control panel and Gracie began biting her lip in anticipation. I winced, expecting fear pheromones to fill the air. To my surprise, though, Gracie was braver than I'd given her credit for. The girl jumped when Sebastien pressed the big red button the first time, but the air between us remained scentless and clear.

"Turn it up, professor," the girl said while I was busy flaring nostrils and sucking in scents. "I *really* need that scholarship."

And, in a blaze of tearing regret, I realized what motivated the child. Gracie possessed no pack mates ready and willing to fund her higher education, boasted no relatives who would fall all over themselves to ensure her every need was met. Instead, the poor human was strapped down in an electric chair, paying her way through college by dint of her own physical pain.

Abruptly, I'd had enough. There were other options, I just knew it. If nothing else, I'd ask Wolfie to create a scholarship just for this girl—the joy of cobbling together his own amusing acronym would more than make up for the loss of cash from our community coffers. Regardless of the eventual methodology, I was confident my pack leader would ensure this pup wasn't forced to shock herself through college ever again.

Placing a supportive hand on Gracie's wrist, I glared at the professor. "That's enough."

"But Gracie said to turn it up," Sebastien answered, fingers twisting the dial higher even as his mouth voiced the words. And for a moment, I froze, hardly believing that even one-body society would be so cruel as to think this was acceptable behavior.

While I hesitated, the professor's finger reached toward the red button for the sixth time that day. And I should have lunged forward to stop him. Should have responded like any ordinary human being and used my physical body to halt the madness.

But the shocks, in the past, had been instantaneous and I wasn't sure I'd be able to come between Sebastien's finger and the instigating button before current began to flow. So rather than considering the fact that most humans weren't even sensitive enough to notice a werewolf's command, I allowed an alpha compulsion to roll off my lips.

"Stop," I ordered. Then I watched as unexpected delight filled Sebastien's mahogany eyes.

Chapter 21

At the same moment, Gracie began to laugh. The student's merriment was so honest and joyful that it would have been contagious...if my wolf hadn't currently been attempting to crawl out of my skin and rip out Sebastien's throat, that is. As it was, though, I needed several seconds to even make sense of my companion's subsequent words.

"You're such a lightweight," the girl told me, pulling electrodes off her skin as she hopped off the chair. "Most people make it up to ten 'shocks' before they give in." Air quotes completed, Gracie turned to drag a box of candy off the shelf behind her back, then rummaged inside to come up with four options. "Here. Which one do you want?"

I gazed at the girl in befuddlement. I was a lightweight...and now it was time for candy?

"It's just *pretend*," the pup explained, shaking the crinkly-coated chocolate bars to catch my attention. "No electricity, no pain. I'm the professor's lab assistant this summer. Hard job, but somebody's got to do it."

Silently, I turned to cock my head at Sebastien, struggling to reassess the conversation that had gone before. A moment ago, I'd thought Gracie was a poor waif down on her luck and the professor was a monster using the girl's desperation for the sake of his own experiments. And now...now I wasn't even sure what to think.

I expected glib explanations to roll forth from the professor's lips, but Sebastien appeared nearly as tongue-tied as I was. The human eyed me speculatively, one index finger pressed against his mouth as if he wanted to speak and was struggling to keep unintended words inside. And as I took in his posture, a shiver ran up my spine.

I had a feeling I'd just made a terrible mistake.

Luckily, Gracie was talkative enough for all three of us. "You've probably never taken a psychology course, have you?" she asked. And when I shook my head mutely, the girl launched into a long-winded explanation that my harried brain finally managed to condense into a mostly understandable core.

The experiment—and it *was* an experiment, that much was now clear—had nothing to do with pain tolerances. Instead, Sebastien was gauging my reaction to the situation, determining how far I was willing to go when both other participants were supposedly on board with creating supposed agony in the pup.

"This project is funded by DARPA, isn't it?" I said at last, drawing conclusions that were perhaps too far-reaching and perhaps a little paranoid...but that felt entirely right at the time.

Because, despite the pretty words Gracie had used to class up her explanation, this didn't seem like the sort of experimentation a civilian organization would care to have their name attached to. And, of the funding organizations listed on various posters running down the hall, DARPA was the clear choice for creation of such an inhumane scheme.

"Yes," Sebastien admitted, speaking carefully as if afraid to set me off...as well he might be since my teeth were bared and I was barely holding back a menacing growl. "It's true that DARPA provided some of the baseline funding. But they support thousands of projects around the globe, and this experiment was and is entirely under my control. Look, I'm sorry we lied to you, but what you took part in today is just a slight twist on the classic analysis of reactions to authority figures. The Milgram experiment...."

Werewolf-like, the male reached out to place one soothing palm atop my forearm as he spoke, and I immediately lost track of all words. Because contact with Sebastien felt like heaven. Like being wrapped up in my family's protective embrace...while diving out of an airplane with only one small parachute strapped to my back. I could almost sense wind whipping against my cheeks, could nearly hear the whisper of a pack mate begging me to pull the ripcord and slow my plummeting descent.

But my usually mild-mannered wolf fought against any attempt to step away from the human's side, instead keeping us stuck in heart-pounding free fall. *Mine,* the beast growled silently, freezing our joint muscles into place.

She and I were usually so closely attuned that I didn't differentiate between our wishes. Sometimes we were wolf and sometimes we were human, but the distinction had more to do with which set of muscles would best achieve our goals rather than it did with any battle of ego or will.

Now, though, we each struggled to take control, fighting for command of a body we usually shared equally. I clenched my teeth and strained against her efforts...and I might just have lost had the ringing of my phone not provided a wolf-friendly excuse for us both to step aside.

Pack is calling, I reminded her. Pack, the one thing that every wolf understood deep within her bones. And, reluctantly, my own inner beast accepted my retreat from Sebastien's touch, allowing me to dig into my pocket for the chiming telephone before turning away to break all contact with the confusing college professor standing by our side.

Then I forgot Sebastien's magnetic attraction as nearly incoherent apologizes filled my ear. "I'm sorry. I'm sorry. I'm *so* sorry."

And just like that, I dropped back down to the hard pavement of reality with a nearly audible thud.

AT FIRST, THE VOICE on the other end of the line was so garbled and confused that I couldn't even figure out who it was. Only after I pulled the device away from my ear and glanced at the screen did I realize this was Lissa, one of the shifters left in charge of guarding my sister's house.

Immediately, my stomach made a beeline for the hard tile floor, but this time for a far less palatable reason than enjoying an enticing human's touch. Because I was sorely afraid that anything Lissa might be so vehemently sorry about wasn't something I wanted to hear.

But I *needed* to hear what was going on...and soon if Harmony's life lay in the balance as I currently suspected. *"Stop groveling and start explaining,"* I commanded, not bothering to take the time to soothe the other female's fears in the human way. Instead, ignoring the other inhabitants of the lab, I unleashed my inner wolf and allowed the beast to carry our human body toward the building's exit, first at a walk then at a trot.

On the other end of the line, Lissa gulped then obeyed. "We watched the apartment all day just like Andrea told us to," the guard started, her voice still quavering but her words significantly more understandable as my compulsion did its work. "No one of Ms. Garcia's description left and no werewolves entered on our watch. But you sounded extremely concerned when you called, so Marcia went to check out the human's hallway. And an old lady came to the door...."

My lips tried to turn upwards into a smile as Lissa painted a picture of the eldest Garcia attempting to chase two Greenbriar werewolves out of her hallway with that ever-present cane. But I could guess where this story was going...and there would be no happy ending to smile about. So I cut into the stream of chatter yet again.

"*Tell me,*" I ordered, forcing Lissa to cut to the chase.

For a moment, even an alpha compulsion wasn't enough to break through the pained silence lying cold and hard between us. Then, at last, Lissa spoke, her words nearly too quiet to hear. "They were gone," she whispered, the pain of a wolf who'd failed her alpha strong even if her voice remained muted and weak. "The human and her pup left before we even got there. They went to the zoo early this morning...and they never came back."

Chapter 22

I was halfway down the block, analyzing the density of nearby shrubbery and trying to decide where I could safely shift, when a sleek black sports car pulled up by my side. "Hop in," Sebastien greeted me, reaching across the passenger seat to push open the gleaming front door.

And even though I needed a ride, I hesitated. The professor's vehicle was the perfect way to get across town as quickly and efficiently as possible...but I couldn't afford to tip my hand further to someone who'd proven himself far more perspicacious than the average one-body. Shifter politics aside, I didn't dare drag this human into the altercation that was soon to come either.

The car looked fast, though. And the human, I had to assume, would be ditchable before any werewolves came into view.

"We don't have anything to talk about," I told the professor...but I nonetheless slipped inside the waiting vehicle. And even though my own unaccustomed rudeness grated on my ears, I found myself unable to mitigate the words with further small talk. Not when my wolf barely allowed me to snap the seat belt into place before forcing our spine to take a hard left turn toward the enticing human in the driver's seat.

Ours, the wolf whispered, filling my mind with a far-too-vivid image of myself wriggling into the space between Sebastien and the steering wheel, letting my shirt ruck up so his chest rubbed against my bare skin. In the wolf's animalistic understanding, it was entirely irrelevant that giving the professor an unrequested lap dance was likely to cause the vehicle we sat inside to wreck. Trying to argue the complete and utter inappropriateness of the gesture was also a recipe for failure, so I didn't attempt to make either point.

Instead, I merely shushed my inner animal while plugging an address into the vehicle's GPS. Not the zoo's coordinates, of course—I couldn't risk Sebastien following me into a showdown that I suspected would turn into a blood bath at my first misstep. But I'd killed time during lulls at the coffee shop researching outings Rosie might enjoy, and the children's museum lay only half a mile away from the zoo's side gate. I could easily hoof it that short distance...and there were plenty of distractions in between to help shake a tenacious human off my tail.

Predictably, my wolf took offense at the idea of running away from a male she would have vastly preferred reaching toward. But when she opened our shared mouth to say something I was sure we'd later regret, Sebastien's aroma coated our tongue and sidetracked the beast from any ill-advised speech.

Our companion's scent was different than it had been just an hour earlier. Equally as enticing, but darker and more bitter, as if the human understood as well as I did that his supposed experiment had harmed the tenuous bond forming between us.

But despite the regret hanging heavy in the air, Sebastien didn't open with an apology when he finally spoke. Instead, keeping his gaze firmly riveted on the road, the male beside me cleared his throat loudly. Then he shattered the ounce of equilibrium I'd managed to rebuild since losing my cool inside the clinical interior of his lab.

"Derek is your brother," the professor said, eyes glinting as they drifted over to catch my reaction. "Isn't he?"

THE SHOCK OF HEARING my sibling's name roll off a human tongue forced words out of my mouth that I immediately wished could be taken back. "How did you know?" I demanded.

And while I half expected my wolf to growl protest of my curtness, she instead turned quiescent beneath our shared skin. Because, attraction or no attraction, family came first. And if this male had harmed our brother...well, I just hoped I could make it out of the car before my wolf skinned our driver alive.

Perhaps the professor sensed the shift in mood, or maybe he just regretted dropping his verbal bomb with such a profound lack of subtlety. Either way, skin around his mouth tightened as the car merged onto the freeway. And after waiting for three long seconds, I was forced to prod in search of a reply.

"Professor...?" I prompted, trying to sound polite even as I fingered the mostly clean knife strapped against my bare thigh.

The tiniest hint of a smile came into my companion's face then, and he shook his head slowly from side to side. "I thought you looked familiar when I first met you," he began, answering my question but also apparently thinking through an issue he hadn't previously attempted to put into words. "Derek was just as cagey as you are when I first ran into him at the bus station. And, in the lab.... Well, I've never experienced anything like that, except with Derek...and you."

I wanted to pounce on the "was" he'd placed so close to my brother's name, but instead I forced myself to cover my butt and smooth over the human's final point first. Just my luck that the one time I'd slapped a compulsion onto a human, the one-body in question was both sensitive enough to notice and scientific enough to be intrigued. "In the lab?" I offered in lieu of an explanation. "I'm not sure what you mean...."

"Okay," Sebastien answered, dropping the topic far too readily for my peace of mind. "So the...tingle...or whatever...was all in my imagination. But you *do* look like him. The hair and the nose and something around your eyes."

You're cuter, though, my companion's scent insinuated, and I had to force myself not to respond to the attraction thrumming back to life between us. Now wasn't the time to be derailed by fickle hormones.

"Where's my brother?" I demanded instead, reminding myself that this human might have been the last person to see Derek before he went missing. Had my sibling fallen into the trap presented by the professor's kindly face and interested manner? Had he revealed too much and ended up as an unwilling test subject in a government laboratory?

As tempting as it was to blame Derek's absence on this human, though, I had a bad feeling that my brother's fate had been his own darn fault. In which case, Derek might not only be a lone wolf but also the worst of werewolf offenders—a traitor I'd be forced to kill on sight.

Shivering, I reached over to turn off the AC.

"I have no clue where Derek is," Sebastien answered, apparently oblivious to my own internal struggle as he broke into my thoughts. But even though he was finally offering information without further prodding, my wolf's ears pricked up as she returned to full alert. Because for the first time since meeting him, we could taste the distinctive odor of an acridly scented lie rolling off Sebastien's formerly enticing skin.

So the professor *was* part of the problem. Disillusionment bit into my skin like the pang of a torn-off band-aid, and I was too upset to feign subtlety this time around. Instead, I barely managed to keep the alpha compulsion out of my voice as I gritted out a repeat of my initial question. "Where...is...he?"

In response, the car skidded slightly as it bumped up against a curb, and a horn sounded off to our left. The intensity of our preceding conversation had prevented me from noticing that we'd exited the highway and entered the downtown area, but I guessed that we were now no more than a couple of miles from my intended destination.

That obliviousness was something I needed to fix. A warring werewolf didn't last long if she lost track of her surroundings.

My hand hovered over the door latch as rush-hour gridlock slowed the surrounding traffic—and Sebastien's car—to a crawl. *I ought to step out now*, I thought, *and leave this human behind.* Harmony's absence turned my spine ramrod stiff while the threat to Rosie's future was a spider-crawl of tension skittering across my skin. Even on two human feet, I could easily reach my sister in a few short minutes if I exited the vehicle now....

And yet...once I left his side, I'd never see Sebastien again. Because the professor was too clever for me to safely cultivate, regardless of our budding connection. He was already on track to figure out that Derek and I weren't your average one-bodies. Meanwhile, his government affiliations made any potential realization far more dangerous than it might otherwise have been.

No, this was my last opportunity to dislodge answers. So, forcing myself to sink back into the car's soft leather seats, I ignored the snail's pace of the traffic around us and instead bored my gaze into the side of Sebastien's head. "Are you really going to leave me dangling, thinking my brother may be dead?" I asked, allowing myself to sound just as young and wounded as that scenario made me feel. I wasn't a defenseless damsel...but I could play one on TV. "Please, just *tell* me what you know."

For one agonizing moment, I thought Sebastien might not comply. But then he turned the wheel rapidly, pulling the vehicle into the entrance of an underground parking garage. Not bothering to hunt out an empty spot, my companion merely screeched to a halt in the middle of the aisle and swiveled around in his seat so we were facing. Only a few inches of heated air now separated our eyes and skin.

"Ember, I really, honestly don't know where your brother is," Sebastien told me, his voice rich with both contrition and truth. The professor swallowed, then continued. "I can't give you an address or even a city...but I do know it's probably my fault that he ended up there."

Chapter 23

Humans love the dark. Being unable to look into a companion's face gives them an entirely unwarranted belief in anonymity...and Sebastien was no exception to that rule. So, like a church-goer shielded from view by the confessional, as soon as the headlights went dim my companion's story came pouring forth.

"Your brother showed up on a Greyhound bus two years ago," Sebastien told me, his voice steady in the darkness. He glanced toward me, providing an opening in which I might explain the familial mode of transportation. But I merely shook my head rather than taking the bait.

Because I couldn't tell my companion that moving vehicles were exempted from the territorial rules governing werewolves. That my brother and I had both felt safe within those metal walls while passing through land owned by other packs. Off the bus, on the other hand...I doubted a lone male shifter would have been welcomed into the heart of the Greenbriar clan with the same open-armed generosity I'd recently been granted as a pack-affiliated female.

"And you picked him up?" I asked instead, nudging Sebastien's story beyond what I suspected would be the first of many disclosures my wolf wanted to share but that my rational human brain forced us to sidestep.

Sebastien nodded in agreement, his eyes searching my face in the near darkness. Then a sigh gusted out as he accepted my evasion for what it was. "I handed your brother a business card just like the one I gave you. Told him about the candy bars and the cash. Unlike most of my subjects, Derek seemed more interested in the latter than the former."

And this I could explain...at least tangentially. "My brother lived pretty close to the poverty line," I murmured, shivering as I realized I'd joined Sebastien in referring to my sibling in the past tense.

"I don't think he's dead," the professor interjected so quickly that it almost felt as if he'd read my mind. One large, male hand stretched toward me, and I itched to accept the consolation physical contact would provide.

But, instead, I tamped down my inner wolf's urges and glanced the other way, effectively cutting my companion's offer of solace off. "Where do you think he is then?" I asked instead. Even to my ears, my voice sounded hard and cold.

For a long moment, no one spoke. Then the professor answered my spoken question while ignoring the undercurrents flowing beneath. "It's complicated," Sebastien told me. "During your brother's first experimental session at the college, I felt something *strange* happening when Derek shut the shocks down."

My nostrils flared as I took in the scent filling the car. Discomfort, curiosity, worry. Not so different from the feelings currently running through my own body in fact.

"I was intrigued by the sensation," Sebastien continued after a moment. "So even though it wasn't really appropriate, I hired your brother under the table and let him stay on my couch for a while. He seemed to need somewhere to sleep, and my house is really too big for one person."

A good home, my wolf interjected. For a moment, I didn't understand what she was referring to. But then, abruptly, I could envision my companion's living room in all its book-lined glory.

Because Derek had called once from a place that looked less like a hostel and more like a home. Shelves and plants competed for pride of place along brightly painted walls, tweaking my inherent curiosity. And before I could think better of the question, I'd found myself asking my brother who he was crashing with.

I realized the error of my ways immediately, of course. Because my brother failed to give a straight answer to my simple question, instead setting off on an extended tangent that told me nothing except that I'd crossed an improper line. For three days after that, Derek hadn't answered my chat requests. But when he'd returned, the lapse was forgotten, my question never spoken of again. He'd even provided a PO address to send a care package to later that month—a compromise from a shifter who was unwilling to let even his sister know where he currently denned.

It had hurt to confirm how little Derek trusted me, and I now sensed that Sebastien had been equally stung by my brother's failure to confide in his pro bono house-mate. But while I could understand Sebastien's regret, there were more important matters at stake. Matters like my brother's safety and continuing existence. So, ignoring the human's bowed shoulders, I continued to nibble around the edges of Derek's unexplained absence.

"You gave my brother room and board so you could study him," I guessed. It wouldn't have been a formal experiment. No, Sebastien was far too clever for that. But if he placed Derek in situations that would tempt the latter to spill alpha compulsions then subtly monitored the results...well, what human scientist wouldn't be thrilled by the opportunity to explore such inexplicable behavior?

"I was too fascinated not to," Sebastien admitted, the scent of old books—the tell of his intellectual curiosity—once again filling the air. "But then I made the ultimate mistake."

Now we were getting to the heart of the matter. I clenched my hands together, hoping the professor would say he'd scared my brother away with a lapse much like my own verbal faux pas. But I knew that wasn't the case. Not when the scent of guilt was now so thick in the atmosphere that I almost choked on my companion's unspoken words.

"You contacted your funders," I suggested, filling the extended silence with words my companion seemed unable to spit out. "You told DARPA about this test subject that made you feel...what...all tingly inside?"

"Something like that." Sebastien laughed, but it was an embarrassed chuckle rather than any indication of true amusement. "I mentioned Derek's name in my usual monthly summary. And, the next day, your brother failed to show up for dinner. I waited a week, then had to admit the truth. My test subject had disappeared without a trace."

HE'S GONE.

For a long moment, I sat in stunned silence, trying to wrap my head around complete and utter failure. Because I'd been willing to leave my pack behind and fight the Greenbriar clan for permission to hunt my brother within their territory. I'd kept my options open to travel even further afield, had envisioned sniffing along Derek's trail and rambling from pack to pack if necessary until I finally tracked my little brother down.

But going up against the human government? At some point, even a wolf has to admit she's been beaten.

It's not supposed to end this way. Because Derek was my *blood*, dammit. I could feel the connection in my soul even if our bond couldn't be explained away using my rational human mind. Losing my only sibling before I'd so much as felt the touch of his bare hand against mine...the concept was so foreign as to be unthinkable.

Two and a half days earlier, I certainly hadn't been thinking about the possibility for failure. Instead, rolling my suitcase up to the waiting bus at dawn had felt like embarking on a brand new adventure while the butterflies in my stomach originated from excitement rather than dread. As a result, I hadn't even looked over my shoulder when dozens of pack mates called fond farewells toward my retreating back.

Now, in contrast, all I wanted was to run home to Haven with my tail between my legs. I'd hole up in my cottage, pulling the covers up over my face and pretending the outside world didn't exist. Or maybe it would feel better to pound my head against the wall until the pain outside matched the agony of losing a brother I'd come so far to meet. I was willing to leave my options open and play the mourning period by ear.

Because, either way, the end would be the same. Once my pack mates decided I'd enjoyed enough solitude to soothe the cavity in my gut, they'd come to call in ones, twos, and half dozens. I'd fix us all cups of rich hot chocolate and let tears salt the frothy drink. Eventually, my loss would be forgotten amid the scents and sights of home.

Even though I was currently located hundreds of miles outside Haven, I was still tempted to curl up inside those fond memories. To let the present and future fend for themselves while I drifted back into the rose-tinted past.

But my wolf's predatory hunger gnawed at my belly, and the increasingly adamant buzz of my phone jolted me awake. *The call*, my inner beast urged. *Our pack.*

Take it then, I countered, not quite willing to relinquish the seductive allure of an imaginary homecoming. The bus ride home would give Wolfie enough time to bake me another masterpiece, and Mom would welcome me with open arms. We'd go running in lupine form as soon as the sun set, would explore our mountainside in search of prey that put this city's measly deer and elk to shame.

This time when my wolf broke into my pity party, she didn't bother with human words. Instead, seizing control of our shared body, she pulled the buzzing phone out of our pocket with a predator's intensity and swiped the screen alight.

And for one long moment, we hung in suspended animation. I tried to tiptoe back toward my self-pitying solitude...while the wolf struggled to read a message that didn't quite make sense to her dyslexic lupine brain.

In the end, curiosity drew me in just as my inner beast had known it would. The amorphous letters my wolf was peering at so intently materialized into words before my very eyes. And the resulting message slapped me in the face with its reminder that Derek wasn't the only innocent whose safety currently hung in the balance.

Top Dog: "Dinner venue has been changed. Dress is informal. Your presence is required immediately."

And beneath the curt invitation came a familiar street number. *The zoo.* Could it be mere coincidence that Chief Greenbriar was summoning me to the same location in which Harmony and her daughter had recently disappeared? I somehow doubted as much.

Chapter 24

Immediately, I lost the final vestige of lassitude as my mind kicked back into gear. Male shifters were attacking women in Chief Greenbriar's own city. At least one of them was doing so using alpha compulsion that the male shouldn't have been strong enough to wield.

Meanwhile, the alpha's mate was well aware of the problem, as evidenced by Andrea's choice to bring my potential rapist along on our morning meet and greet. Surely what Andrea knew, her spouse knew as well...which suggested the latter was implicitly supporting what was not only an ethical lapse but also a potentially earth-shattering breach of shifter security.

I'd gotten sidetracked down a blind alley earlier trying to figure out what could prompt a strong alpha werewolf to allow such shenanigans to go on under his very nose. Chief Greenbriar was no pushover, no pack leader clinging to power by the skin of his teeth. So why look the other way when his underlings' actions threatened the shroud we'd so carefully drawn over our very existence? Why risk his entire pack—and werewolves everywhere—for the sake of a few males who could easily be barked into line?

"He didn't ignore it. He *caused* it." I only realized I'd spoken aloud...and walked halfway across the parking garage...when a car door slammed behind me and the human professor called after my rapidly retreating form.

"Wait! We can figure this out together. Whatever happened to your brother is my fault, and I'll do anything I have to in order to fix what I broke."

Nice thought. Sweet thought. And, at its heart, such a very *human* thought.

"It's too late," I called back, turning my head slightly so the words would carry...but not allowing myself to set eyes on a male who strummed at my heartstrings as if they were stretched across the barrel of a banjo. Instead, I pushed a modicum of alpha compulsion into my final response, hoping the order would stick. "*Go home.*"

Sebastien wasn't a shifter, though, so my command didn't push him backwards with unerring gravity. Instead, footsteps continued in my wake as I tore down the ramp and out into the darkening city. The clatter of shoes on pavement dogged my heels as street lights flickered to life above both of our heads, and the sound impinged on the cheerful chatter marking the post-work rituals that were the closest human beings came to pack life.

Deep within my belly, my wolf whined her confusion. It shouldn't *hurt* this much to walk away from a human we barely knew. It shouldn't feel like we were ripping our heart out of our very chest when we ducked into a blind alley, clambered up onto a brick wall, and flattened ourselves atop a shadowed awning while waiting for our follower to pass unwittingly by.

Unfortunately, Sebastien was a more than adequate hunter despite lacking a lupine skin. So rather than following the false track I'd presented, the professor paused beneath my perch and stared down the empty lane toward the only sign of life—a stray cat jumping up onto the lip of a dumpster in preparation to dine. The professor might be facing in the wrong direction, but he knew when he'd lost a trail.

For a long moment after that, the human merely stood silently, pupils dilating against the deepening gloom. Then he murmured into the empty air. "Ember, please don't disappear like your brother did."

The words would have been inaudible to a human standing further than five feet from his current position. But I was a wolf, and I heard every syllable.

I heard every syllable...and I knew I couldn't respond. So, slithering up onto the nearest rooftop, I rose to my feet and padded away on silent hunters' feet.

Because Harmony and Rosie were in danger two blocks to the west. And while I'd failed my brother, I refused to let down the rest of his small but deeply important pack.

AS SOON AS I LEFT SEBASTIEN'S side, a sharp jolt of pain cut through my belly. And the churning grew worse rather than better as I made my way across a series of darkened rooftops, leaving the professor further and further behind.

Only when I'd descended back to street level at the midpoint of my journey did I find something more interesting than cramping to capture my attention. There, stomach troubles were quickly forgotten as rigid hairs on the back of my neck suggested I was being watched.

Spinning in a tight circle, wolf-assisted senses took in the subtle clues hanging in the evening air. The faintest aroma of shifter proved that a member of Chief Greenbriar's pack had passed this way within the last half hour, and the faintest tinge of fear coated my tongue like mud. Still, no one accosted me as I strode onward through streets that appeared completely devoid of life. Even the zoo—which rose out of the darkness as a long line of cast-iron fencing—had descended into nighttime silence.

The side gate, though, wasn't locked tight for the evening as it should have been. Instead, one half of the ten-foot-tall barrier swung in the breeze, the opening inviting me forward like the sight of a gingerbread cottage had drawn Hansel and Gretel out of the woods and into the witch's lair.

Unlike those unwitting children, I knew I was making a mistake by diving in without spending appropriate time on reconnaissance. And yet....the ache in my stomach was making it difficult to think while the faintest gasp of a baby in the distance sped my feet rather than slowing them down. If I hesitated too long and allowed harm to come to Rosie in the interim...was that really worth the safety of my own skin?

I was through the gate before I'd even made a conscious decision to continue forward. And as soon as I stepped through the gap, words came whispering in around me, encircling my skin like a confounding fog.

"Find a mate. Find an appropriate female mate. Find a mate and settle down. Settle down and make some pups."

I shook my head to dislodge the noise, glancing up at the speakers that dotted the top of the monkey habitat off to the left. Had Chief Greenbriar tapped into the zoo's PA system? Because that *was* the alpha's voice layering additional tension onto the roiling of my gut.

"Find a mate," the refrain began again, growing neither softer nor louder as I padded deeper into the quiet zoo. I stalked past the reptile habitat—locked up tight—then wandered alongside sleeping giraffes and elephants.

There was still no sign of two-legged life, though. So when the pathway split, I made an educated guess and followed the most likely direction. After all, what shifter wouldn't naturally gravitate toward real live wolves?

"Find a mate. Find an appropriate female mate. Find a mate and settle down. Settle down and make some pups."

Despite my best attempts to keep my wits about me, the compulsion to breed built as I traveled deeper into the animal habitats. First, it was just an easily ignorable hunger that reminded me of the craving for chocolate. But then I found myself salivating over an educational poster on the side of the penguin enclosure, eying a two-dimensional woman's cloth-covered curves as if she represented the most delectable croissant from a Paris cafe despite my formerly relentless heterosexuality.

I could handle the siren call of a poster—barely. But then the scent of an ovulating human slipped inside my flaring nostrils. The female had sat on this exact same bench only an hour earlier, had risen and walked out into the city alone. Perhaps if I turned west and picked up my pace, I could find the breeder before someone else took her to mate....?

Okay, this is bullshit. Sticking fingers into my ears did nothing to break the compulsion's hold, but closing my eyes and holding my nose helped a little. The obsession eased yet further when my wolf rose up to join me in guiding our shared body down the path, her simple mind keeping more complex human emotions at bay.

The compulsion is coming via the Greenbriar pack bond, I realized at last, my wolf's assistance lending me sufficient breathing room to analyze the effect rationally. Which meant Chief Greenbriar was more powerful than I'd originally imagined, his ability to compel behavior from pack mates at a distance something I'd never run into before.

Perhaps that explained the apparently civilized males driven to rape females along this city's tree-lined streets? If so, then one of those potential rapists might have been given leave to wield his alpha's power in the process, the pack leader's compulsion being sufficient to freeze my feet in place when the male in question shouldn't have been powerful enough to even stare me down.

I shivered, wondering what would lie at the epicenter of these insidious commands. Because if a female like me with no interest in members of the same sex was being so easily manipulated by the alpha's compulsion, then what chance did male members of his own clan have against the endlessly repeated refrain?

"Find a mate. Find an appropriate female mate. Find a mate and settle down. Settle down and make some pups."

Once again, my skin itched with the urge to obey. My hands dropped back to my sides in an attempt to speed my walking...and then, above the deep rumble of Chief Greenbriar's voice, came the thready wail of a fussy child.

My niece.

Forgetting both caution and compulsion, I changed trajectory so Rosie's voice guided me forward. Then I let the wolf have her head as our human feet broke into a run.

Chapter 25

"There she is, the guest of the hour."

Chief Greenbriar was dressed every bit as formally as he had been the evening before, and the tux he wore should have looked out of place along the dusty paths of the overpopulated wolf habitat. But, instead, I almost imagined the animals had invited him over for dinner and were even now whipping up a feast within their shadowed cavern...rather than cowering in the far corner hoping to escape from a predator twice as dangerous as themselves.

"Alpha," I acknowledged, advancing slowly so I had time to scan the surroundings in search of the child who had initially drawn me in. At first, I couldn't find her. But then Harmony's arm twitched and I caught sight of mother and daughter huddled together beneath a spreading maple tree at the edge of the enclosure.

I heaved a sigh of relief...then sucked the same recently exhaled breath right back in. Because what I'd taken for a tussock of browned grasses at the humans' feet now turned its head toward me, eyes glowing forth above a slender snout. Harmony and Rosie hadn't chosen the tree as a safe harbor in a dangerous storm. Instead, they were being herded and guarded by a territorial wolf.

Or rather, a territorial *were*wolf. Because the unmistakable aroma of shifter emanated not just from Chief Greenbriar, but from his lackey as well.

And while the realization that this beast was governed by human emotions might otherwise have calmed my nerves, the alpha's compulsion was still reverberating within my own skull. Sure enough, the wolf's teeth were bared and his gaze was intent upon the thin-skinned innocents who huddled so close to his pointed fangs. Whether or not the male's human intellect was awake and active behind those shadowed eyes, the animal could be summed up in a single word—dangerous.

For their parts, Harmony and Rosie were terrified. Human fear spread across the enclosure like a suffocating smog, and it was all I could do to prevent my wolf from carrying me directly to my family members' aid. Instead, I walked up to the fence line separating me from both alpha and hostages and tried to act casual as I leaned against its metal railing.

"You asked me to come and I came. Now I'd appreciate it if you released these humans into my care."

Harmony's already stuttering breathing caught in response to my speech and I winced, realizing what I'd said. Unfortunately, my sister-in-law was no dummy. She'd been herded here by humans, wolves, or some subset of both...and in the process she must have discovered the existence of monsters that sometimes wore humanity's skin. My words had just lumped me in with the monsters instead of the humans. I somehow doubted Harmony would willingly parole herself into my care any time soon.

Not that my sister's release appeared immediately imminent. "You know the law," Chief Greenbriar answered, breaking through my regret like a hot knife through cold butter. "These humans have become privy to information they shouldn't have ever known. As such, their fate is predetermined. But that's not why we're here...."

Once again, the refrain from earlier rose up through my thoughts. *"Find a mate. Find an appropriate female mate. Find a mate and settle down. Settle down and make some pups."*

And as I strained against the mental intrusion, I caught the faintest flicker of movement along the path from whence I'd come. Barely managing to keep Harmony and Chief Greenbriar in view at the same time, I swiveled to look behind me...and caught sight of two shifters stumbling out of the shadows that lined the concrete path.

Aaron came first, back ramrod-stiff as he fought his father's compulsion and nearly stumbled over his own feet in the process. I apparently wasn't the only one whose head was filled with sexual orders, either. Because as soon as the male took in my existence, his eyes lit up and his mouth dropped open while drool began sliding down the side of his slackening face.

Charming.

Meanwhile, Roger slunk out of the darkness with more attentiveness to his current surroundings. This second male's jaw was clenched, and he reached one hand toward his significant other before shaking his head and allowing the arm in question to fall back against his side.

And as Roger advanced yet further into the light, I realized the reason for his hesitation. Because one eye was ringed with purple bruising while a cut leaked blood at the corner of his brow. The two had struggled already, I gathered, probably initially against Chief Greenbriar's orders then later—once Aaron fell under his father's sway—amongst themselves.

In the end, though, alpha compulsion had won out over the restraint of a lover. So Roger had found no solution save trailing along in his partner's wake. He, like I, had been drawn here in an effort to save someone he held dear, and he, like I, now waited impotently to see what the pack leader had in mind.

"Son, welcome," Chief Greenbriar greeted Aaron, either ignoring or failing to notice the other recently arrived werewolf. Now that his offspring was present, in fact, the older male stepped down from the mound he'd used to elevate himself above the fray, striding forward and unlatching the enclosure's gate before extending one arm toward the entrance as if to usher us all inside. "I've selected two fine specimens for you to choose from," he told his son proudly. "Tonight will be a very special night."

Whatever his personal feelings on the matter, Aaron had no choice but to obey. Jerky movements suggested the heir apparent was fighting against his alpha, but legs carried him forward through the open gate anyway.

For his part, Chief Greenbriar led his son back into the wolf habitat without concern for the two other shifters—Roger and myself—who could easily have leapt upon his unprotected back. We all knew who had the upper hand here and who was no more than an audience for the upcoming charade.

"Find a mate. Find an appropriate female mate. Find a mate and settle down. Settle down and make some pups."

For a split second, Roger and I united in our joint rejection of the stifling command. Our eyes met across the intervening space, and I thought the male might try something profoundly stupid. How easy would it be to end the craziness by spilling Chief Greenbriar's blood across the grass?

But we weren't wolves. We were people. And, after a split second, my companion's lips pursed as he turned to trail along in his lover's wake.

Which left me alone on the other side of the heavy metal gate. Steeling my courage, I followed my companions into the jaws of Chief Greenbriar's waiting trap.

Chapter 26

R osie caught sight of me as soon as I passed beneath the half-strength lamp at the entrance to the enclosure. "Kak, kak, kak," the toddler crowed, hands waving wildly as she abruptly lost interest in the menacing wolf at her mother's feet. Apparently, Auntie Cake was more interesting than a predator who could have swallowed one of the child's limbs in a single gulp.

For her part, Harmony met my gaze steadily despite my recent verbal lapse. *Protect my child*, she as good as said into the intervening air, dark eyes flashing with the fervor of a desperate mother. And my feet obeyed the silent plea, thrusting me forward across the uneven ground in an ill-fated attempt to protect my blood.

Chief Greenbriar, on the other hand, offered no leeway for me to complete my mission. *"Ember, join us,"* he ordered, the overt command turning me away from my original trajectory until I was being pulled up onto the knoll the alpha and his son had so recently ascended. Now Roger was the only one lagging behind in the enclosure's shadows, and I held out little hope that the male in question would make a move to protect my family when his gaze remained firmly fixed on the younger male by my own side.

Stage set to his satisfaction, Chief Greenbriar dismissed non-relatives as beneath his concern and turned his attention fully upon his only son. "This is the spot where your mother and I pledged our troth," the older male began, gracing Aaron with a toothy grin that struck me as more than a little un-hinged.

Then the alpha's tone turned honey sweet as he reminisced about events that had occurred before the rest of us were even born. "Andrea and I mated in the wolf pen," the alpha mur-mured, "to prove that our wolves would always be at the fore-front of our partnership." He paused, stared up at the stars, then closed his eyes dreamily. "And that choice has served our clan well. We've led this pack for thirty long years, and never once has an enemy breeched our borders."

Chief Greenbriar is living in a dream world, I realized, tens-ing as I imagined using the alpha's distraction to assist in my es-cape. But before I could begin prying my feet out of the com-pulsion that held them stickily in place, the older male's eyes cleared and he leaned toward his son once more.

"Soon," Chief Greenbriar continued, the snarl of a wolf re-turning to his tone, "it will be your turn to make the sacrifices necessary to guide our people into the future. It's time for you to make the proper choice and decide for the good of our pack."

Then beneath the male's audible words, that familiar re-frain rose in volume, circling again through my aching head. *"Find a mate. Find an appropriate female mate. Find a mate and settle down. Settle down and make some pups."*

Both words and yearning were the same ones that had pushed against my skin ever since I entered the zoological park.

But now they impacted me differently. After all, for the first time since becoming affected by Chief Greenbriar's compulsion, there *was* a living female present for the urge to latch onto. And I found myself craving Harmony's touch with every fiber of my being.

The intensity of the pressure, in fact, twisted my body around to face my sister even as feet that had been ordered to stay put brought me up short. A grunt from Aaron suggested the alpha's son had slammed up against a similar obstacle. Unfortunately, no such impediment stood between Roger and his goal.

I tried and failed to yell a warning. But Harmony had no eyes for the male who had attacked her two nights earlier and who now lunged forward with lupine grace but on flat human feet. Instead, her face paled as her own guard broke with shifter law and sentenced my sister to death by surging upward into the form of a man.

"An appropriate female mate," the guard growled, his words seeming to emanate from the body of the wolf he'd recently left behind. Then, batting Rosie's questing hands aside, hard fingers closed around Harmony's quivering arm.

"Mine," the male intoned, his final word dripping with lust.

I WATCHED IN HORROR, my muscles unwilling to even strain now and my lungs forgetting to breathe. There was nothing I could do to stop the depredations about to occur. Nothing except watch in horror as the wave that had carried us all toward Harmony broke over each of our heads.

Overwhelming pressure stifled our collective breathing for one split second. I was not only unable to move, I could almost feel my bones melting inside my skin as my vision hazed out. Only my wolf's steadfast presence held me erect....

Then the pressure was retreating back into the distance from which it had come. The tension in my muscles eased. Harmony's guard remembered his humanity and turned aside to block his prisoner's scent from flaring nostrils. And as quickly as it had come, the danger dissipated into thin air.

Unfortunately, the alpha's secondary compulsion took advantage of my momentary relaxation to slap me back into line. Legs and torso twisted unbidden until only eyes maintained contact with Harmony. Then even that connection faded until my sister and niece were once more invisible behind my rigid back.

And now, at last, my attention returned to the closer tableau that resembled nothing so much as a human wedding ceremony. Chief Greenbriar was the officiant, elevated atop a rock that generations of wolf feet had worn smooth. On his left side, Aaron—rumpled clothing, angry eyes, and all—was obviously the groom.

And despite my own sugar-streaked attire, there was only one conclusion I could make about my part in the upcoming farce. I wasn't the wedding-cake baker or the caterer—my preferred roles at such an event. Instead, my stance mirrored Aaron's, my location making my own part disappointingly obvious.

I was the bride.

Chief Greenbriar had even wrangled a sufficient audience to make our mating official from a human point of view. Roger and the unnamed shifter stood close enough to see but too far away to take part—witnesses. And behind their backs, I caught the first glimpse of moonlit eyes as wild wolves crept out of their cavern to form a ring around us, providing the additional spectators that Chief Greenbriar clearly craved.

The beasts hovering in the shadows lacked humanity and boasted long teeth and nails. But they weren't the reason my heart pounded and my breath drew short. Instead, I found myself running through every possible escape route in an effort to avoid the upcoming ceremony...and coming up short.

There was no way out. A few short words were all that would be required to bind me to a mate and a pack I had no intention of calling my own. Words that Chief Greenbriar could easily coerce into existence. Words that then couldn't be truly broken until my own death.

"Find a mate," the silent voice whispered beneath my increasingly scattered thoughts. *"Find an appropriate female mate. Find a mate and settle down. Settle down and make some pups."*

Then—mood set—Chief Greenbriar pierced me with a pack leader's relentless gaze before returning his attention to his only son. "The moon is full," the alpha said ceremoniously into the air between us, "and the night is young. Soon we'll run. But first, the mating ritual must be complete."

Chapter 27

To my surprise, Aaron was the one who jumped into this opening with his first real offensive move to date. "Dad, you don't want to do this...." the younger male began, hands clenching into fists as he fought the compulsion that held us all in place.

Down in the long grasses below, Roger's eyes locked with those of his lover. And for a moment, I thought Aaron might be able to utilize his partner's strength to break free of his father's commands. After all, there was fortitude in blueberries, Roger's chosen dessert. Maybe that same tenacity would be enough to wiggle Aaron out from under the alpha's thumb....

But even that thread of possibility snapped as Chief Greenbriar's intention alone silenced his errant son's complaints. "You're wrong," Chief Greenbriar countered. "This is exactly what I want to do."

Then the older male's heavy hands whipped out, pressing me and Aaron together until our shoulders touched. "I've waited long enough for my son to do his duty," the older man intoned. "This clan craves a crown princess and a new heir on the way. It's time and past time for you to put childish yearnings aside and to choose your mate for the sake of the pack."

Meanwhile, the alpha's unspoken words continued to whirl through the air between us. *Find a mate. Find an appropriate female mate. Find a mate and settle down. Settle down and make some pups.*"

This time, though, the words slunk beneath the thin armor presented by my Haven mantle and sunk their teeth into my unprotected skin. I realized a moment too late that my white-knuckled grip on familial protection had slipped. And now Chief Greenbriar's compulsion took advantage of that lapse to seep into my veins and run through my body like blood.

A mate, I thought, head cocked. I need a mate.

Meanwhile, Aaron's gaze latched onto mine as he also gave up the struggle. The heir apparent had tried to force his father to see reason, had tried to use Roger's bond to fight against the older male's instructions. But, in the end, neither defense turned out to be enough. Aaron had surrendered to the inevitable...and so, at last, had I.

"*Find a mate. Find an appropriate female mate. Find a mate and settle down. Settle down and make some pups.*"

My intended reached out across the small space that divided us, taking my unresisting hand into his own. He was virile, I noticed now. Strong and handsome. Our blood would merge well together, creating offspring capable of leading the Greenbriar pack into a brighter future. Widening my mouth, I smiled at the vision of family soon to come.

But my mate didn't speak. Instead, he cocked his head and waited for me to make my move. "Tradition," Aaron whispered after a long pause, reminding me that the female werewolf was the one to initiate the mating pledge.

And Chief Greenbriar—despite having used compulsions to enforce our arrival—observed the proprieties as well. The alpha waited silently for the better part of a minute, night turning darker around us as I opened my mouth in preparation for the requisite words to emerge.

Only my tongue refused to twist into sound. My vocal cords remained resolutely silent. I no longer remembered *why* I was resisting. Couldn't recall any reason not to bond myself permanently to this prime specimen of manhood who stood with head cocked waiting for me to make the first move.

Still, something told me to wait. Something told me I needed to touch base with my family before I made this unalterable choice. So I strained with every fiber of my being to find the tether connecting me to my home pack. I could do this, I knew...even though the Haven thread was currently so deeply hidden that it might as well have snapped and dissipated into thin air.

Nonetheless, I trusted that my pack's joint strength was somewhere out there waiting to be tapped, waiting to remind me why I wasn't yet ready to embrace my Greenbriar future. And for a second, I thought I'd found the safety net my family represented. I smelled Wolfie's distinctive aroma of pine needles and leaf mold, and I reached out with incorporeal fingers to snag the connection...

...only to have the tether slip through my fingers as Chief Greenbriar's patience abruptly ran thin. *"Ember, choose your mate,"* the older male commanded me, his compulsion so strong it nearly sent me tumbling to my knees.

My ears began to ring as I lost track of what I was trying to do. Didn't I want a mate? Wasn't there an appropriate male ready and willing and only eighteen inches away from my nose?

Like Aaron, I was now past the point of no return. Past the point of railing at the fates or scheming for a way around my apparent future.

Instead, I opened my mouth. And I chose the partner who would determine my clan, my future, and my happiness for the rest of my natural-born life.

"MY MATE..." I GULPED then licked my lips as further words failed to materialize. Two feet away, Aaron's blueberry eyes bored into my own and the thready growl of a werewolf's complaint rose from the heir apparent's partner as Roger padded two steps closer to our elevated mound.

Meanwhile, the wild wolves moved in tighter as well. There were at least a dozen animals present, and their scents suggested each one was half crazed from domesticity. But despite the imminent danger, a single huff of breath from the Greenbriar alpha returned shifter and animal attention alike to the task at hand.

"Ember," Chief Greenbriar prompted, not bothering to raise his voice or fully reiterate his command this time. After all, he didn't need to. The previous words hung heavy in the air between us, my skin attempting to peel away from the underlying bones as I used every tactic I could think of to delay...and failed.

"My mate," I began again, closing my eyes to block out the sight of the darkened zoo. And, to my surprise, the evasive maneuver worked. Because the darkness beneath my lids wasn't entirely black this time around. Instead, thin threads of light popped into existence, most so tenuous as to be nearly invisible but two brightening by the moment as Haven pack mates managed to bridge the gap that stood between us.

The bond was too weak to protect me from Chief Greenbriar's overt compulsion, but the connection was just enough to kick my faltering brain back into gear. In response, I grabbed the literal breathing room with both hands and sucked in the reluctant scent of my intended, the anger of his true partner, Rosie's chubby toddler sweetness, and the faintest hint of Harmony's floral shampoo.

I can't mate with Aaron. Reality washed over me like a cup of scalding coffee, and with it came the understanding that I needed to act fast. Because at any minute, the Greenbriar pack leader would break with tradition and force his son to make the first move...in which case I'd be even more stuck than I already was.

After all, if the stories I'd heard were true, then the only thing worse than a mate bond built like a bridge between two disinterested parties was *half* of a mate bond. The tether would slap in every breeze, dragging us to and fro against our will. I'd turn my head...and accidentally force Aaron to walk into traffic. He'd scratch his nose...and my own finger would poke me in the eye.

The reality of my current situation felt like a car-sized cast-iron skillet balanced atop my head. I needed to make a decision immediately. Either accept the inevitable and mate with this male or somehow close off that possibility before Aaron could begin to speak.

Which means, I realized even as my mouth gaped open against my will, *that I need to choose a* different *mate.*

The flash of brilliance blinded me...then revealed, in its afterglow, an avalanche of fatal flaws. If anyone in my home pack had possessed even an iota of possibility as mate material, I would have dragged the unfortunate werewolf to the altar long since. There simply wasn't any mate beyond Aaron on the metaphorical table.

Wrong, my wolf whispered. *Easy,* she told me. *Just look.*

But look where? I'd searched for mates for the better part of the last decade. I'd hunted high and low and found nothing...within the bounds of Haven, at least.

Because my cousins, despite our lack of shared blood, were far too family-like to become mates. Instead, I'd dated a few drifters. But it had been easy to let those go once they wandered beyond Haven's borders. None was worth a second glance.

Beneath my skin, my wolf growled out wordless lupine exasperation. Until now, she'd been hanging back, attempting to understand the muddle of human maneuvering that had washed around us. But *mate* she understood. *Mate* was a concept she could sink her teeth into.

Allow me, the beast said with the lupine equivalent of steely politeness as she pushed me gently yet forcibly out of the way. Then, moving my tongue without permission, my animal half spoke words I somehow knew in my heart to be true.

"My mate," she said—we said— "now and forever...my mate is Sebastien Carter, human professor and holder of my heart."

Chapter 28

The nagging pain that had followed me ever since leaving the professor's side disappeared in an instant...and in its place a tearing agony of loss forced a cry from my lips. The sensation was akin to losing a leg to a shark or ripping out my own entrails with jagged fingernails...except, I'd have to say my current agony was far, far worse.

In response, I glanced down, half expecting to find blood squirting out of my femoral artery as the ground rose up to meet my face. But I was still standing erect and the night-darkened grasses appeared just as dry and unsullied as ever beneath my feet. No, this desperate ache hadn't resulted from a physical injury that I'd been so oblivious as to miss.

On the other hand, the summer air had turned so cold against my skin that I could barely prevent chattering teeth from taking off my tongue. My head swam as the moon abruptly transitioned into two moons within the evening sky. And I breathed too quickly, oxygen supersaturating my blood as my wolf clued me in to what had been lost.

The Haven bond. Our pack. They're gone.

My inner animal's reminder was silent...and even so, the words slurred as if she could barely force her thoughts to coalesce into linear form. Not wanting to believe, I squeezed my eyes further shut and reached into the darkness of my mind with ephemeral fingers. The pack tethers had always been there, just out of sight. I couldn't believe the seemingly ironclad bonds could ever disappear entirely.

First and foremost, my link to Wolfie—father, alpha, and cupcake-decorator extraordinaire—should have been so thick and strong it wrapped itself around my wrist like a friendly boa constrictor. And beyond that familiar foundation, there would be other connections present as well, dozens of life forces interwoven into a rope so strong it never let me drop to the cold, hard ground.

But my grasping hands found nothing. Just emptiness, darkness, and a cold that seemed to permeate my very soul.

Which begged the question—without those invisible threads, without my family...did I even truly exist?

I tried to rein in my terror, to remind myself that I'd known this would happen from the get-go. Rationally, I'd understood that whoever I mated with would determine which pack I eventually called my own.

If I mated with Aaron, I'd become a Greenbriar. The obvious corollary, though, was far less palatable now that it had become a reality. If mating with a pack wolf would draw me into his clan, then mating with packless Sebastien left me attached to...well...nothing, I guessed.

I shivered, trying to find another answer beyond the one that currently stared me in the face. No matter what I'd thought would happen, I hadn't expected the transition to be so quick. So sharp. So final.

Squaring my jaw, I tried to force my scattered thoughts back onto the task at hand. The connection couldn't have disappeared completely, I decided. So, with wolf-like attention to detail, I hunted for *any* bond at all. The Greenbriar mantle—borrowed and soon to be cast off—would be sufficient to buoy me up until I worked this minor problem out. I'd draw against that alpha's power and soothe my shattered soul...then I'd find a way to rebuild what had been so recently left behind.

Because I couldn't afford to lose my family. I refused to break ties with mother and father and cousins and uncles and aunts who meant more to me than life itself.

There was no way I could extricate myself when I knew each family member's favorite flavors and colors, their foibles and strengths. My calendar included every birth date along with which nights each pack mate might need a friendly shoulder to lean on. And, in return, my closest companions knew the exact same facts about me.

I just have to search a little harder. A one-way mating bond probably acts like the borrowed Greenbriar mantle—hiding what's still there underneath. Mating to Sebastien won't have cut off the connection entirely. It will have just driven my basic connections deeper so they're harder to find.

But I knew even as I formed the words inside my mind that they were, each and every one, desperate lies. Because there was nothing inside me to be found. No borrowed weight like the one that had sat lightly upon my shoulders for the last two days, no iron-clad connection attaching me to the Haven pack within which I'd grown from pup to adult. Instead, searching fingertips found only one lax thread leading out from my soul...a thread that gave way beneath my tugging as if the knot on the other end had never been fully tied.

And as I pulled against the slack, I opened my eyes and saw not the zoo but the inside of Sebastien's vehicle. Around me—around him—the fancy sports car was illuminated only by the glow of buttons and dials. Meanwhile, the professor's emotions hung heavy in the air, a fog of exhaustion and disappointment combined with the barest sliver of niggling guilt.

For a moment, I relaxed into my mate's imagined proximity. Then, far too quickly, he *sensed* me there, hovering behind his eyeballs.

In response, our shared head cocked to one side as Sebastien's voice filled the small space. *"Ember?"* he asked into the night.

My mate felt me...but he was also entirely human and had no idea how to complete a mating ritual even when the unattached tether was slapping him in the face. Plus, who said the professor *would* bond with me even if he was able? We'd barely spent two hours in each others' company during a similar number of days and had never heard of the other before that. It would have been crazy to consider forming a partnership on such short acquaintance when a true mating bond lingered for the rest of a being's life.

It would have been crazy...unless the decision was the last gasp of a desperate werewolf who didn't want to harm anyone except herself.

Then our shared eyes blinked and my connection to Sebastien was broken. In my belly, my wolf circled uncomfortably, whining at the absence of our mate. Meanwhile, down by my hip, the adamant chime of a cell phone demanded my immediate attention.

RELUCTANTLY, I OPENED my eyes and reached for the phone. Because even though I could no longer feel the current caller attached to my very soul, I could guess who this would be—Dad. The shattered pack bond would have forced my father to jump to an entirely warranted—if thankfully incorrect—conclusion. No way would I punish Wolfie by making him think that his only daughter had left the Haven clan the most likely way...by growing stone, cold dead.

Unfortunately, wrangling the cell phone out of my pocket was easier said than done. My breath came in gasps, I wasn't so sure I could speak, and I was absolutely certain I needed to be somewhere else. My skin prickled with the urge to run toward my absent mate even as my rational brain reminded me that a very angry alpha hovered inches away from my unprotected neck.

Oh yeah—and then there was that unnamed shifter who held similar control over my sister and niece. Plus wild wolves inching closer by the moment. Details, details.

Despite the danger swirling through the air around us, I refused to be responsible for Wolfie's rampage if I failed to accept his call. So I forced fingers to behave long enough to answer, then I pressed the cool plastic against my ear as I attempted to turn pained grunts into actual words.

"I can't talk now, Dad. But I'm alive," I told him quickly. Then, duty done, I ended the call and gazed at last upon the alpha whose growl had formed a counterpoint to the flurry of terrified questions running through my own mind.

"You made the wrong choice," the alpha in question rumbled. But he didn't pounce. Instead, he punished me in a way far worse than ripping the still-beating heart out of my heaving chest. "Bring the backup female closer," he called over one shoulder, not bothering to imbue the words with any alpha power.

Within seconds, Harmony was standing at the foot of the hill peering up at us, she and her daughter both leaning away from the naked shifter who'd threatened them in the recent past. For his part, the male relegated his hands to the non-erogenous zone of Harmony's hunched shoulders although his eyes remained avariciously trained upon my sister's fabric-covered breasts.

Rather than remarking upon the scent of inappropriate lust filling the air, Chief Greenbriar turned once more toward his son. And this time he failed to give Aaron any leeway, instead spitting out a stark alpha command. "*Aaron, it's time for you to stop stalling and to choose your mate.*"

Energy filled the air as the compulsion took hold. But my wolf hummed her approval as she realized what had gone unnoticed by our puppet master—that, this time around, the Greenbriar alpha had seriously missed his mark.

Maybe the pack leader expected his previous compulsion to keep "female" and "appropriate" and "pups" at the forefront of his offspring's mind. Or maybe, somewhere deep down inside his subconscious, the alpha just wanted his son to be happy. Whatever the reason, I saw the moment Aaron noticed the lapse, saw the spark of joy filling the younger male's eyes as he opened his mouth and hurried through a choice that, in a perfect world, shouldn't have been rushed.

"My mate," Aaron said, his words both loud and joyful as they rang through the dark night air, "is Roger Jones."

Then, out of the shadows, another male mimicked his partner's words, nearly stumbling over his consonants in his haste to beat Chief Greenbriar to the punch. "And my mate is Aaron Greenbriar. I claim you now and forever, Aaron, as the only partner of my heart."

Just like that, the air filled with the scent of roses as the duo's mate bond clicked firmly into place. It was done. Aaron and I were both mated...only not to each other.

Chapter 29

The aftermath was beautiful. The newly-formed tether materialized so strongly as to be nearly visible, its breathless perfection filling the void in my own gut for one split second...before leaving me even emptier than before.

And in response to that cavern of need, my inner wolf stole my volition and pushed us away from the wedding mound in search of our own mate. Or at least she tried to. But despite strained muscles, our feet remained just as firmly planted as they had been five minutes earlier...

...until, that is, the compulsion freezing us in place shattered so quickly I nearly fell forward onto my face. Meanwhile, a female voice rang out from the still-open gateway at the edge of the enclosure. "You didn't invite me to my own son's wedding?" Andrea demanded, stepping out of the shadows in a sequin-studded evening gown that looked like it had been made to reflect the moonlight.

And maybe the outfit had. Because the region's second-in-command possessed a flare for the dramatic, one she was currently putting to very good use. The sweetness of honeysuckle whirled around me so strongly that I was certain Andrea had supplemented her signature aroma by chemical means, and the click of heels against concrete drew every eye in her direction as she stalked toward us as slowly as any hunter.

Meanwhile, the wolves encircling the mound began to pull back one by one, padding over to sniff at the newcomer's legs and hands. In Andrea's shoes, I would have been daunted by the proximity of wild teeth and claws—after all, most werewolves had no particular ability to communicate with beasts. But Andrea allowed and even encouraged their familiarity, trailing her fingertips along one animal's spine before turning to glare in her mate's direction.

"You harmed our son. You harmed our pack. *You* are the rot at the Greenbriar core," she intoned coldly.

And as much as I would have liked to stay and watch Chief Greenbriar receive his comeuppance, I had more important matters on my mind. So, backing away from the nearly visible anger that flowed between the mated pair, I slipped down the opposite side of the mound and padded over to my sister.

"This one is *mine*," I murmured, meeting the guard's eyes with the full force of my inner wolf. And while the male in question would have fought against my forwardness at any other moment, the electricity sparking between the pack's first- and second-in-command froze the other shifter relentlessly in place. Due to his pack connections, he was unable to so much as growl a retort.

I, on the other hand, wasn't currently hindered by the Greenbriar mantle...or any other sort of one. So ignoring the sharp pain shooting through my gut, I took advantage of my own broken pack bonds to drag Harmony away from her befuddled guard.

"Kak, kak, kak!" Rosie chanted, grabbing hold of my hair and pulling painfully as soon as I came within reach. The tears in my eyes, however, were more closely allied to joy than to discomfort. Because merely standing alongside relatives eased the pain in my stomach ever so slightly and reminded me that—pack bond or no pack bond—I wasn't entirely alone.

Andrea and her mate, on the other hand, were becoming more alone by the moment. Shifters couldn't divorce in the human sense. Instead, if they ever chose to sever their mating bond, the resulting discomfort was akin to that catalyzed by an alpha compulsion...only with the effects multiplied by a thousand and lasting for a lifetime.

Despite the agonizing consequences, Andrea had so chosen. Even from my current distance, I could *feel* the Greenbriar bond ripping apart, the sensation so powerful that secondhand spillover was nearly enough to send me to my knees. Wincing, I struggled to keep my stomach contents inside me where they belonged even as I drew Harmony toward the open gate as quickly as possible.

And I wasn't the only one affected. "Mom, don't!" Aaron began, his voice strangled as if his tongue was fighting against a mouthful of toffee.

For a split second, the sensation of being torn asunder eased ever so slightly, allowing us all to breathe. Then: *"Aaron, Roger, Edgar, go,"* the female intoned, putting enough force behind her words to send the remaining members of her pack scurrying toward the looming gate. Following their lead, I met my sister's questioning gaze with a shrug then picked up my heels to accelerate our own retreat.

Because, behind our backs, the growl and shuffle of angry wolves was growing louder by the second. And the air once again filled with an emotion so intense it made my ears pop.

"You've turned into a wolf, so it's only appropriate that I throw you to the wolves," Andrea murmured to her mate. Or perhaps I should say to her *ex*-mate. Because the female's most intrinsic bond was gone, and I could only imagine the pain that must be tearing through her body at the loss of her other half.

There was only one way to ease that shooting pain, and Andrea was blood-thirsty enough to take it. I half expected Chief Greenbriar to fight back. But instead, there was only a single pained grunt as the first wild animal struck. Then the scent of blood followed us all the way to the gate.

Chapter 30

We'd escaped the worst of the preceding danger virtually unscathed. And yet...the instant Harmony, Rosie, and I burst through the zoo's gates to find my parents' car waiting at the curb, tears started leaking from my stinging eyes.

Terra and Wolfie had come for me. Despite my insistence that I needed no help. Despite the danger involved in invading another alpha's territory. Despite the broken pack bond that meant I was no longer a Haven wolf. All of those reasons aside, my parents had tracked me down and now waited patiently to pick up the pieces.

Well, not so patiently. Mom was the one behind the steering wheel—a seriously good thing for everyone's sake since letting Wolfie drive was tantamount to assisting in vehicular homicide. Which meant Dad was closer to me, his hand pushing the passenger-side door open the instant I emerged from the shadows at the entrance of the zoo.

"No!" I called, eyes drying as I realized we weren't out of danger quite yet. Because whoever won the Greenbriar power struggle tonight, I had a sinking suspicion the new alpha would be sniffing this pavement first thing in the morning, seeking any sign that Wolfie had broken pack law by setting foot outside the neutral territory of his car.

Luckily, Wolfie's feet halted just before they touched down on open pavement....although the male continued to menace all and sundry with a thready growl. For her part, Mom's hand landed on her mate's shoulder in an attempt to placate him, but she clearly wasn't confident of her own abilities to restrain my father's over-protective streak. Instead, Terra jerked her chin and widened her eyes at me from behind her mate's back. "Get over here before your dad blows a blood vessel," she commanded even as her eyes said *"Welcome! I love you! Thank goodness my daughter is safe!"*

Obeying her request as quickly as possible, I released Harmony's hand and hastened to Wolfie's side. "Dad, calm down," I said placatingly as I sprinted forward.

Even as I spoke, though, I knew my words would do little good. What Wolfie really needed—and what I gave him as soon as I was close enough to touch—was the sensation of my palm sliding across his stubbled cheek, my warm skin proof that I wasn't a ghost. "I'm alive, I'm okay, and I appreciate the help," I murmured into Wolfie's waiting ear.

I *was* alive, but even as I made a move to open the back door of the car, I doubled over in agony. "Kak?" Rosie called in concern, then Harmony's warm hand slipped around my waist in an effort to pull me back erect.

The human's willingness to come in contact with someone who'd recently admitted to being a werewolf was surprising. But even more surprising was the way my own gut-wrenching agony eased ever so slightly beneath my sister's touch.

Unfortunately, lack of pain allowed my brain to kick back into gear once again. And as it did so, I realized that I wouldn't be able to flee in my father's car. Not without Sebastien, not tonight, and possibly not never.

Because the mate bond I'd offered to an unsuspecting human was still very much in play. From the feel of things, I might be able to stretch our tether far enough to hit the other side of downtown, but that was about it. Despite the fact that the professor considered me no more than an interesting test subject, I was apparently stuck traveling no further than a few short miles from my life partner's home base for the foreseeable future.

And as my eyes rose to meet my father's, I could tell that Wolfie already understood that I wouldn't be able to rejoin the family in Haven today. He understood...and the pain of our separation was the reason Wolfie had descended into his instinctive animal brain even as he remained solidly situated within his human skin.

"Can you take Harmony and her family back to Haven to keep them safe?" I whispered through a swollen throat that threatened my ability to speak. Across the pavement, my gaze met that of my sister, and this time Harmony bowed to a necessity she'd rejected just the day before.

"Just let me text my mother," the other female said quietly in response to a question I hadn't even voiced aloud.

And, for a moment, I couldn't help but smile. The Garcia matriarch wouldn't be happy about being asked to den with werewolves. I could almost see the old woman stomping around the family's small apartment, packing bare necessities and preparing to meet her daughter and granddaughter in time to make their grand escape.

A grand escape that required the support of my parents, of course. Parents I'd left seriously out of the loop. So perhaps my sister wasn't out of the woods quite yet....

TURNING BACK AROUND to face Terra and Wolfie, I realized that these bedrock foundations of my existence didn't even know who Harmony was, didn't have a clue that my brother had fathered a pup whose mother was unaware of shifters' existence until earlier this evening. The details of that particular soap opera would take hours to properly tease out. But as I opened my mouth to provide the cliff-notes version, my father's humanity glowed back to life behind glittering eyes.

"Your pack is our pack," Wolfie promised, reaching behind him to push open the back door and make a place for guests within the cluttered back seats.

"We'll stop for a car seat along the way," Terra added, stretching out to take my sister's hand in both of her own. Female eyes met, questioned, matched. And, just like that, my sister and niece were folded into the Haven clan.

I, on the other hand, found my feet growing colder by the second as my former buffers against packlessness—Harmony and Rosie—were encircled by my parents' love. I swallowed with some difficulty, then forced myself to meet Dad's eyes at last. "I'm not sure when I'll be able to come home..." I started.

But Wolfie didn't allow me to say words that would only break both of our hearts. Instead, he rifled around in the debris at his feet, then came up with a cardboard box that he handed over as proudly as if he was offering a crown to a new monarch. The courtliness was strange given words on the exterior proving that the container had begun life enclosing a takeout burger. Still, a sniff test promised sweeter contents inside.

I cracked the lid then tears began leaking from my eyes yet again as I realized Dad had made me another cupcake. Somehow, in the midst of driving hundreds of miles north, waiting for phone calls that never came, and hacking into a cell phone's GPS data to determine my current location, Wolfie had carved out sufficient time and space to bake fatherly love into a treat to be delivered by his endlessly affectionate hands.

"You two are such softies," Mom said from the other side of the center console. She reached across, wiping away my tears with the pad of one thumb, then smiled fondly as she elaborated. "You should have seen your father in that hotel-room kitchen. Every time the bond went wonky, your dad threw flour at the ceiling or clawed up the counter. We had to pay extra for damages when we checked out."

And, just as Terra had intended, the image of my half-wild werewolf-baker father *was* enough to dry my eyes and bring me back down to planet earth. Meanwhile, Dad had gathered his own composure more closely about him before pressing his larger palms around mine—one atop the box and the other beneath my extended hand.

"Bond or no bond, you're welcome at home whenever you choose to come," Wolfie told me as the heat from his touch refilled a tiny portion of the gaping hole that had dug itself into my belly earlier in the evening. "In the meantime, eat this cupcake when you need a boost. And let me know when you land somewhere safe and sound."

"I will," I promised, agreeing to everything even though I had no idea where I would spend the night or even whether I would ever be safe again.

Then Harmony's cell phone rang and the sound of irate Spanish filled the evening air. Rosie exploded into another round of "Kak, kak, kak!" And Harmony attempted to soothe both the older and the younger generations while gazing upon my parents with hooded eyes. Despite her earlier agreement, I could tell my sister wasn't quite convinced that her best way forward was to enter a car full of strangers with her daughter on her hip.

"Later, Mama," my sister said at last, clicking off the phone and standing uncertainly beside the still-open car door. The human's muscles tensed, and for a moment I thought Harmony might grab her daughter and run...right into Andrea's unfriendly arms.

"I know everything you've seen tonight is crazy...." I started. I wasn't sure how to fix what had been broken between us sufficiently to get my sister into the car, but I did know I couldn't let her run off into certain danger.

To my surprise, Harmony didn't need further convincing. Instead, she pulled me in for a tight embrace that felt like the first sip of hot chocolate after walking miles through February snow. "Find your brother," my companion whispered into my waiting ear. "And I'll be alright."

Then Rosie was wailing at being ignored and my sister drew back to soothe her. Jiggling the child into good humor, the pair slid together into the back seat.

My parents' farewells were similarly fond but brief. Then car doors slammed, the engine roared to life, and brake lights glowed red as the final remnants of my pack faded away into the night.

For my part, I was left standing there in silence, chewing upon Harmony's final words. Because I'd thought there were no stones left unturned surrounding Derek's disappearance...but my sister's faith in his continued existence suggested that perhaps I'd given up too soon.

"What am I missing?" I murmured, fingering the key that sat cold and hard in my pocket. And as I racked my brain, my memory finally turned up the missing piece.

Chapter 31

"**D**onuts," I'd suggested twelve months earlier, not bothering to gaze into my cell-phone screen as I lounged on the sofa and ribbed my little brother about his favorite dessert—a mystery he'd yet to elucidate a year into our long-distance relationship.

"Because I look so sweet and fluffy, right?" Derek countered, a growl in his voice. Still, I knew my only sibling well enough by this point to be certain he was amused. So I refused to relent.

Grabbing the phone in one hand, I carried our connection into the adjoining kitchen and started pulling ingredients off the shelves with the other. *"Oatmeal cookies? Vanilla pudding? Ooh, I know,"* I teased. *"Pecan pie...."*

"...because deep down inside I'm really a nut," Derek finished for me. His laughter was real this time around, a rarity from a male who always maintained a tough exterior even around his doting older sister.

In response, I gazed into the screen, enjoying this rare moment of solidarity. Behind Derek's lanky form, plants draped around a sun-lit window, and the worry that always gnawed at my gut when I thought about my brother's secretive nature eased. He was safe, he was happy. And, finally, he was in my life...virtually at least.

"I just want to feed you," I said, only realizing I'd spoken aloud when emotions too numerous to count flitted across my brother's usually closed-down face. Biting my lip, I prepared to backpedal. Better that than give Derek yet another chance to retreat the way he'd done every other time I'd tried to draw him closer to my home pack.

Only, this time around, my timing must have been spot-on. Derek smiled back, eyes appearing older than my own despite the fact that I had a few years on him, but his stance otherwise remaining uncharacteristically relaxed. *"How about a PO box?"* my sibling suggested after a few seconds. *"I'm not staying here long so the address is only temporary. But if you really, really have to mail me a...."*

Derek paused, even then unwilling to relinquish such an important secret as his favorite flavor. *"A moonpie?"* I suggested, batting my eyelashes as I named the very last dessert Derek might possibly enjoy. My brother was definitely not a lovey-dovey marshmallow sort of guy.

"Not a moonpie," Derek growled. *"I'll text you the address even though you're a pest. But it's temporary. Tem-por-ary. Got it?"*

"Yes, sir!" I answered, saluting smartly. And, behind my back, I'd crossed my fingers, hoping this was the first step toward meeting face to face. I wanted nothing more than to give Derek a hug...and a safe place to call his own.

Still, a momentary sugar rush would have to suffice for now. To that end, I'd put together an assortment of varied desserts, hoping to hit the nail on the head with one of them at least.

But the care package hadn't done the trick. Derek had evaded my questions about which, if any, of the pastries he'd enjoyed. And when I asked whether I could use the same address the next week, Derek told me he'd moved, that his old PO box had been canceled.

That I'd have to eat the subsequent mountain of moonpies by myself.

Now, sliding my brother's key out of my pocket, I realized that Derek *had* changed PO boxes as promised. Because the number etched onto this small metal surface didn't match the one embedded in my memory from twelve months prior. The post office in question had likely changed as well.

Still, I'd bet my last dollar that this was a mail-box key. And I had a feeling I knew which location Derek had chosen for his new stash as well.

My brother's recent mentions of campus, his affiliation with Sebastien...every arrow pointed toward the row of metal boxes I'd walked right past the day before without realizing my brother's secrets might be hidden therein.

Go. Now, my wolf demanded. And I obeyed. Retracing my footsteps into the darkened zoo, I shed clothes and knives, cupcake and phone before rolling my possessions up as carefully as I could into the stained and ripped blouse that had seen better days. Then, using my bra to bind the ungainly bundle around my chest tightly enough that it would stay put even in lupine form, I relaxed into my wolf.

It had been too long since we'd run four-legged, and the night was terribly empty of other pack mates. So I couldn't resist lifting my head and belting out a mournful howl bound to make human neighbors roll over in their soft, snug beds.

Then, putting my nose to the pavement and using my wolf's direction sense to guide us, we took to our heels and we ran.

THE COLLEGE ADMINISTRATION building was locked up tight, but someone had forgotten to close a window on the eastern end. Leaping through the small aperture was easy in lupine form, after which I shifted in order to access the hall.

And even though I was anxious to discover whether the newest clue would bring me any closer to my missing brother, I toed the line anyway and wasted thirty seconds donning human clothes. Or, rather, donning *most* of them. Because it appeared that somewhere between the zoo and the college, my clever bra luggage carrier had slipped, with the result that I'd lost something quite important—my only pair of pants.

Biting my lips, I eyed the video cameras stationed at intervals along the junction between wall and ceiling. A red dot glowed at the base of each lens, suggesting that the surveillance equipment was fully operational...meaning that anyone noticing my lawless behavior would also get a good long look at my bare bum. To counteract that eventuality, I slid down the length of the hallway with my back to the wall. But then the bay of mailboxes came into view, and I forgot human dignity as I broke into a run.

Which box? Well, that question, at least, was easily answered. The key in my hand had a number etched along one side—404. And, as I turned the key in the lock, I realized that this notation had been another far-too-easily-overlooked clue.

Because Derek gave my father a run for his money in the geekiness department. Even I knew that a 404 error meant an internet address couldn't be found...so why hadn't I made the connection when picking the key out of the dirt during the Greenbriar hunt? I'd assumed my brother was being his usual cagey self and making me flail about for orneriness' sake. Instead, he'd used the number as a hint that he expected to fall off the radar through no fault of his own...and I'd totally missed the reference.

"What's done is done," I murmured, allowing my own failings to flee into the night. Instead, I held my breath as the tiny door in my hands swung open and disclosed my brother's rented space. And there it was—the faintest odor of moss and sawmill lumber promising that Derek had frequented this PO box in the not-too-distant past. *Success.*

The mail room on the other side of the box was dark, but lupine eyes easily picked out the curved shape of a sheet of paper within the intervening space. Removing the box's sole offering, I carried the paper over to a window and read the words printed thereon.

"Box full—please come to the desk during regular office hours to collect your mail."

Seriously? I'd traveled all this way, had finally figured out Derek's elusive clue...and now I'd be required to return and talk to the mail clerk tomorrow because my brother's box had overflowed?

"No, that doesn't make any sense." Retracing my footsteps, I peered inside the small rectangular receptacle once again. It was just large enough for my arm to fit through, not that reaching inside would do me any good. After all, whatever packages or junk mail had originally clogged the small space would be unreachable on the other side of the slender divider. Not even humans were so un-security-conscious as that.

And yet...my wolf forced me to stick my arm inside anyway. What can I say? Animal instincts are seldom willing to leave well enough alone.

And just this once, tenacity turned out to be a positive rather than a negative. Because a protrusion along the top of the box scratched a minuscule wound through the skin of my forearm, and fumbling fingers soon pulled out a thumb drive that had been taped there just out of sight.

"Huh," I murmured, turning the small rectangle of plastic and metal over with questioning fingers. Derek had so much to say that he'd left me an electronic storage device to hold all the data? Not a memory card that I could slip into the back of my phone and access immediately, but a thumb drive that would require a computer to get the information out? Didn't Derek realize I'd left any computer this thumb drive would fit into back home with my own clan?

Of course, campus was full of technology centers. There were publicly accessible labs in every library and dormitory, plus one just a few doors down from the coffee shop where I currently worked. None of the spaces were open on a summer evening...but I *did* know one person who was bound to have a computer close at hand. According to my tangled but very thoroughly present mate bond, the male in question didn't live very far away either.

I could almost feel my wolf howling gleefully beneath my skin. She was finally going to get her way and tighten the tether that ran between us. She was finally going to give Sebastien an opportunity to solidify our bond.

I wasn't so sure about the latter point. Instead, I was purposefully keeping my own expectations low, figuring I'd be happy if Sebastien didn't close the door in my face when I showed up on his doorstep without the benefit of pants.

Chapter 32

As the wolf trots, Sebastien lived only five minutes away from the center of campus. *Smart*, my animal half decided. *Easy commute.*

Despite the short distance, my inner beast had forced us to shift and run here on four fleet feet. And now the wolf was so confident in her imminent acceptance that she padded up onto the darkened porch before I could even suggest a loop around the perimeter to ensure Sebastien was the only one hidden therein.

Because he *was* present. The mate tether told me as much, and so did the light streaming out the downstairs windows. Meanwhile, the porch smelled of nothing but mopping and Sebastien, proving that my mate was the only one currently in residence.

I didn't accede to my wolf's demand and ring the doorbell right away, though. Because I was far less sanguine about being granted permission to enter than was my enthusiastic animal half.

After all, wardrobe malfunction and current furry body aside, Sebastien and I hadn't parted on the best of terms earlier in the evening. The human had admitted his responsibility for getting my brother snatched by DARPA, then I'd run off without any explanation. Wouldn't it be smarter to catch some Zs, lick my metaphorical wounds, and beard the professor in his laboratory tomorrow? If we waited until the morning, I could even bake an apology cupcake to sweeten the pot....

But my wolf rebelled. Wresting control of our shared body out of my human hands, she plunked our butt down onto the floorboards and refused to get back up. At least she hadn't rung the bell in lupine form—evidently, I should be grateful for small mercies.

Okay, I get it, I told my animal half, relinquishing the reins long enough for fur to recede and bare human knees to end up kneeling in front of Sebastien's front door. I could *feel* the professor moving around inside now, awake despite the late hour. The male was ambling aimlessly from room to room, leaving me wondering whether he was as uncomfortable without me present as I was without him.

It was all I could do to prevent my wolf from pushing open the door without concern for clothes then barging inside to join him. Instead, I shook out blouse and underwear that had grown even more repulsive between here and the college, leaves and city grime clinging to every available surface while rips and missing buttons further marred the clothes' structural integrity.

Dad's cupcake was still intact within its protective box, though. And I'd lost neither phone nor knifes. So I guessed it was all good.

Tying the suit jacket around my waist to shield my lack of trousers from view, I ran trembling fingers through hair that saw no more reason to behave than my wolf had done a few moments earlier. Then I laughed at myself for even trying. Sebastien would have to take me as I was, because there was no way I'd be wowing the human with coiffed beauty tonight.

So I was half dressed, filthy, and chuckling at nothing when Sebastien opened the door before I even rang the bell. "Ember?" he asked, blinking owlishly into the darkness.

Maybe human eyes aren't good enough to pick out the minor details, I thought hopefully. Perhaps I could talk to Sebastien here on his doorstep then beat a hasty retreat. Find somewhere safe to clean up before tracking my mate down tomorrow when I looked more human and less like a two-legged wolf.

Except my mate reached behind him to flick a switch, and the abruptly glowing porch light soon illuminated me in all of my scuffed, streaked, and sullied glory.

I expected my mate to recoil. To shut the door in my face, or at least to edge away from a degree of filth that city humans rarely encountered. Instead, he reached out to take my arm.

"What happened to you?" the professor demanded. And as his fingers closed around my bare skin, the contact alone nearly dropped me to my knees.

Instead of succumbing to the seductive allure of our mating bond, though, I merely straightened my shoulders and looked directly into my partner's dark chocolate eyes. "If you invite me in, I'll tell you all about it."

"Then, please," Sebastien answered, "by all means, come in."

From the Author

I hope you enjoyed Huntress Born! If so, the sequel—*Huntress Bound*—is now available. But before you pick up book two, perhaps you'll help lend this title wings by leaving a review?

If you'd rather delve into Haven's past, Terra and Wolfie's first book, *Shiftless*, is free in ebook form on all retailers. You can also download a free starter library when you sign up for my email list at www.aimeeeasterling.com.

Thanks for reading! You are why I write.

Made in the USA
Coppell, TX
10 November 2021

65535297R00125